THE INCREDIBLY
DEAD PETS
OF REX DEXTER

THE INCREDIBLY
DEAD

Disney • HYPERION

LOS ANGELES   NEW YORK

PETS

OF REX DEXTER

AARON REYNOLDS

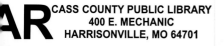

First Edition, April 2020
LSC-C
Printing 3, 2021
FAC-020093-20073
Printed in the United States of America

This book is set in Garth Graphic/Monotype
Designed by Jamie Alloy

Library of Congress Cataloging-in-Publication Data
Names: Reynolds, Aaron.
Title: The incredibly dead pets of Rex Dexter / by Aaron Reynolds.
Description: First edition. • New York : Disney-Hyperion, 2020. • Summary:
Cursed by an old carnival game, sixth-grader Rex Dexter uses his new
ability to communicate with dead animals to investigate the mysterious
deaths of endangered zoo animals.
Identifiers: LCCN 2019019757 • ISBN 9781368051835 (hardcover)
Subjects: • CYAC: Ghosts—Fiction. • Zoo animals—Fiction. • Endangered
species—Fiction. • Blessing and cursing—Fiction. • Schools—Fiction. •
Mystery and detective stories.
Classification: LCC PZ7.R33213 In 2020 • DDC [Fic]—dc23
LC record available at https://lccn.loc.gov/2019019757

Visit www.DisneyBooks.com

To Jodi,
who believed Rex's crazy tale from the start

PROLOGUE

Allow me to be completely transparent. You probably won't believe any of this.

Even my best friend, Darvish, didn't believe me at first. And that guy will believe just about anything.

When we first met in third grade, I told him I was really a spy for the country of Poopsylvania. He believed it for three solid weeks.

You heard right. He believed in a country called *Poopsylvania* for almost a month.

But even Darvish had a hard time choking down recent events in my life.

Which is why I haven't told a single living person what's been happening to me.

Except Darvish. And now you.

Deep breath. Here goes.

I can talk to dead animals.

There. I said it. Are you happy now?

I'm talking about animals that are deceased.

Bereft of life.

No longer with us.

Only, apparently, they are still with us. And let me tell you, they're a chatty group.

I don't know how they find me. I'm not sure who is handing out my address in the animal underworld. But somehow, they do. They find me. They talk to me. They pester me to do stuff for them. I've become an afterlife errand boy.

A word of advice . . . if you ever find yourself in a contest with the Grim Reaper, or a mechanical facsimile of the Grim Reaper, make sure you win.

Perhaps I've said too much. Maybe I should back up and start at the very beginning.

Good idea. Forget you read this.

1

My story starts with a dream. We all have dreams, right? A fire in the belly that drives our spirit toward accomplishment.

George Washington dreamed of being the first president with wooden teeth.

Albert Einstein dreamed of having fluffier hair than any other scientist in history.

Pepto Bismol dreamed of a world without diarrhea.

The first thing you should know about me is this: More than anything else in the world, I've always dreamed of owning a dog. A real-live pet of my own.

I know what you're thinking. *Why a dog? How about a cat? Or a gerbil?*

In my mind, a dog is the only true pet.

A cat? No.

A ferret? Cool, but no.

A gerbil? Please.

Of all the household animals, a dog is the pinnacle. No other animal can compare. And the best of the best? My greatest wish? My most fervent dream? A chocolate Labrador. That's a proper pet.

Don't get me wrong, I'm open to other possibilities. A yellow Labrador would be fine.

A black Labrador, also fine.

Even a golden retriever would be okay. Not perfect, but certainly acceptable.

As you can see, I am not picky.

I was practically born to have a dog. After all, my name is Rex. Rex Dexter. It's a dog's name, for crying out loud. It's one step away from being named Fido. Or Bandit. Or Spot.

With a name like mine, I should obviously own a dog. But I don't.

See this empty backyard? It is devoid of canine.

See the foot of my bed? It suffers from absence of pooch.

See this kitchen floor? It is without dog dish.

It is a sad state of affairs.

My cruel situation is made even worse by a cold and ruthless reality: Everyone I know has a pet.

Everyone.

For example, there's Sami Mulpepper. Sami Mulpepper is the smartest kid in my class. She has wavy hair and smells of soup. She also has an English setter named Sarsaparilla. You can tell she's smart by her choice of pet.

This does not mean I like her. I do not.

Edwin Willoughby sits three rows behind me at school. He has a pit bull named Alfred. I respect his life choices.

Even Holly Creskin has two cats named Tiger and Sardine. Cats don't really count, but it still supports my point. *Two* cats. And I don't think she even likes animals. She wrinkles her nose every time I bring them up.

My own best friend has four dogs, if you can

believe it. *Four.* It is greedy in the extreme. Here is a list of the pets living at Darvish's house:

1. A pug named Rascal
2. A dalmatian named Tikka
3. A schnauzer named Hong Kong Fooey
4. A boxer named Sir Barks-a-Lot
5. A fat raccoon (nameless) that resides in Darvish's yard because his mom leaves dog food on the back porch.

Darvish insists that the raccoon does not count. But even without the raccoon, I think we can all agree: Darvish is a pet hoarder.

One time Darvish let me pretend that Rascal was mine and take him for a walk. He is a thoughtful friend, despite his pet-hogging tendencies.

Five minutes into our walk, Rascal threw up on my shoe.

So I could tell his heart wasn't in it.

2

The closest I've come to the dog of my dreams was Bub. Bub was not the dog of my dreams. That is mostly because he was a fish.

A fish does not count as a real-live pet. But I suppose it is better than nothing.

I had Bub for exactly twenty-seven minutes. His name was supposed to be Bubbles. However, he suffered a very unfortunate mishap just prior to receiving his full legal name.

It wasn't technically my fault.

I was following directions given to me by a licensed professional. The guy at PetPlanet said to put him in water as soon as possible.

Where was I supposed to put him in water?

Do we own a swimming pool? Of course not; my parents are cheap.

Is there a large aquarium in my house that is currently vacant? Don't be ludicrous.

Do I reside on beachfront property? I wish.

There is only one place in our house that is filled with water. So that's where I put him. It was just supposed to be for a second or two.

I was dutifully filling Bub's little fishbowl at the sink. I was saying, "I think I'll call him Bub—" That's when I heard the flush.

Can I help it that my dad doesn't look for fish before he takes care of his business?

After that, my parents decided I was "a little under-responsible" to have a pet. Which is ironic because I might be one of the most mature, responsible, rational people I've ever met.

"What if you had flushed a dog?" my dad said. Which is silly.

First, I did not flush Bub. Any jury of my peers would see this.

Second, it is practically impossible to flush a dog down the toilet.

Unless it's a corgi.

Or a Chihuahua.

I'm pretty sure those are known in the business as the "flushable" breeds.

3

Ms. Yardley is taking attendance.

She is my sixth-grade teacher.

She has a voice that is roughly the same pitch and decibel level as a dead car battery trying to start. I feel for her. For all of us, really.

But, happily, I can't hear it at the moment because Darvish is talking to me.

"I smell chowder," he says. "Do you smell chowder?"

"Of course I smell it," I say. "It's coming from our soup-scented neighbor to the north."

"Canada?"

"No," I explain. "I don't like to be rude, so I will talk in code. Her name rhymes with Clammy Dullpepper."

"Well, whatever it is, it smells good," he says. "Tomatoey."

I refuse to dignify such talk with a response. Everyone knows a true chowder does not contain tomatoes.

Plus, his assertion that Sami smells good is preposterous. Some might say she smells wonderful. Some might say she is highly attractive. Some might say her hair is the magical color of autumn leaves kissed by early morning sunlight. But not me.

"So, are you having a birthday party?" Darvish asks. As my best friend, Darvish is well aware that my birthday is looming. I think this might finally be it: the year of the dog. After all, it has been a couple of years since the Bub fiasco. I am hoping the stink of that unfortunate incident has been washed away by the loofah sponge of time.

"Darvish, birthday parties are for children," I say, shaking my head sadly. "Do I look like a children?"

"Yes," he says. "We both look like children."

"Well, I'm not. And neither are you."

"Okay."

"But you are welcome to come over after I get my presents so I can gloat."

"Okay."

Ms. Yardley's unmistakable voice has reached my row. "Darvish?" calls Ms. Yardley.

We have been in school nearly two months, yet this poor woman still insists on calling daily attendance. I worry there may be something wrong with her memory functions. For her own well-being, I should bring this to the attention of the school board at their next meeting.

"Here, Ms. Yardley!" says Darvish from in front of me.

"Rex?"

I do not answer. It is a little game we play.

"Rex, please say *Here* when I call your name," she says.

"Ms. Yardley," I say, addressing her with the deference due her station. "Please refer to me as 'The Dogless Rex Dexter.'" We've talked about this and she full well knows it.

"I'm not doing that," she says.

I have the feeling my civil liberties are being infringed upon.

"How about 'His Royal Petlessness'?"

This proposal has also been repeatedly met with resistance. "I'm not doing that, either."

"It's not for much longer," I inform her. "I expect to receive that dog any time now."

"Rex . . ."

"My birthday is in a few days," I explain helpfully. "My parents do not realize it, but I have been cutting out pictures of dogs from magazines and leaving them around the house. They have no idea that I'm secretly manipulating them. It's adorable."

"Rex . . ." She sighs, rubbing her eyes.

This tug-of-war has been raging since the start of the school year. "Allow me to suggest a compromise. You may feel free to come up with a name of your own invention, as long as it reflects my ill-treated and petless state and the general unfairness of the world we live in."

"Rex, please."

"Just think, Ms. Yardley. I've allowed you carte blanche. The only limit is your own creativity."

"Rex Dexter . . ." she says through gritted teeth.

"Here." I yield. I cannot fight her forever.

4

The big day has arrived.

My birthday jubilee.

The glorious anniversary of my birth.

B-Day for Me-Day.

I may be too old for a party, but you can never be too old to have cake and ice cream for breakfast. The cake is shaped like a chocolate Labrador (my request). It is also chocolate cake (also my request). With chocolate ice cream.

That's right. A chocolate chocolate chocolate Labrador.

If the thought of that makes your heart take flight, you are not alone. The whole idea is poetic and speaks to the soul as well as the taste buds. If Emily

Dickinson had created chocolate chocolate chocolate Labrador cakes instead of books, she probably would have made a few more sales.

As tasty as this poetic concoction is, the main event beckons.

My mom emerges from the kitchen, heavy laden with my present. She carries a box with a big red ribbon. It has holes on the side.

Holes!

Holes in a box mean one thing and one thing only.

From within the box comes the glorious sound of muffled scratching. My suspicions are confirmed.

There's something alive in that box.

And that something is a living, breathing-air-through-holes-in-a-box DOG!

Clearly, my subtle manipulation of their brain waves these past weeks has paid off.

The size of the box could indicate a small breed. Terrier. Dachshund. Not as big and impressive as one would hope, but I pride myself on being Mr. Flexible. Besides, a small box might also mean a chocolate Labrador *puppy*.

I put my ear to the box and I hear it. Breathing. And an odd little clucking bark. Perhaps some exotic and rare breed? My mom and dad have outdone themselves. Have I mentioned lately that I have the best parents in the known universe?

My anticipation has been pushed past its limits. I cannot wait a moment longer to meet my new lifelong pal and bosom companion.

I rip off the ribbon.

I untie the strings.

I take a deep breath.

Then, at long last, I yank off the box lid to gaze joyfully upon my very own pet . . .

. . . chicken.

Please disregard my previous statement about having the best parents in the known universe. It is not their fault. My parents and I are clearly suffering from a failure to communicate.

Perhaps I've been too subtle with my hinting. I

try to express myself in simple, easy-to-follow terms. "Guys, this is a chicken."

"Exactly!" says my mom.

"What do I do with it?" I ask.

"It's a pet!" says my dad.

"A chicken isn't a pet, Dad. A chicken is a Happy Meal."

"It's a practice pet."

Practice pet?

"This will give you a chance to practice your maturity," says my mom.

"Take good care of the chicken. Then we can see about getting a dog," says my dad.

There is one thing in the world that I wanted for my birthday more than a real-live dog: a lesson in responsibility.

That's sarcasm, by the way.

Bitter birthday sarcasm. Which is the most sarcastic kind of sarcasm known to mankind.

5

"That's definitely not a dog," says Darvish.

"I know it's not a dog."

"I have four dogs," he points out. "So I'm kind of an expert on them."

This greedy kid is forever rubbing his brood of pets in my face.

"And that's definitely not a dog."

We are sitting in my room. Darvish is on my bed, eating a bag of chocolate chips he has produced from his backpack. Just chocolate chips. Who eats a bag of chocolate chips? Darvish, that's who. The kid always has some random snack on him, which is a handy skill set to have available when the munchies kick in.

I, however, am not eating a bag of chocolate chips.

I am busy staring at my new "pet." I suppose it is attractive, as far as poultry goes. It has reddish feathers and a sassy black tail. And that weird red flap on the top of its head. Which probably makes this a rooster, technically speaking.

But despite its regal bearing, this rooster has done nothing but cluck.

Cluck, cluck, cluck.

It has loads to say but nothing of real substance. I think its eyes are even pointing in different directions.

I don't blame my parents. If anything, I blame myself. I really thought I was raising them better than this.

"Do you have any chicken supplies?" asks Darvish.

Up until this exact moment, I have been blissfully unaware of the existence of chicken supplies. I shake my head. "You mean chicken food?"

"Yeah. And a chicken food dish. And a chicken water dish. And a chicken litter box. Whatever chicken stuff that chickens need."

He's right. My parents have given me a practice pet and tossed me into the deep end with no chicken supplies. Those two are wily. But I am onto their games. If I'm going to show the depths of my common sense and responsible nature, I clearly require chicken-related accessories.

It's time for a trip to PetPlanet.

I love PetPlanet because you can bring your own pets into the store with you. Of course, I have never had a pet to bring into PetPlanet before. Bub left this world too soon. I tried to take Rascal there one time, but we all know how that little caper turned out.

But now I have . . .

. . . a chicken. I am going to have to get used to saying that.

"I just realized something," I tell Darvish. "I'm going to walk into PetPlanet with an animal of my very own for the first time ever."

"Your own pet!" he says. "That's kind of exciting for you."

"Well, not a real pet," I clarify. "But a living, breathing animal-shaped companion."

"I've done it loads of times with Rascal. It's no big deal."

"Life holds so few perks," I say. "Quit ruining this for me."

"Sorry," he says. "How are you going to get your chicken there?"

He's right again. I have no chicken collar. (Item #1 on the shopping list: chicken collar.)

And I have no chicken leash. (Item #2.) So I tie a piece of rope around my chicken's neck.

Well, I try. This chicken is having none of it. It jumps up on the bed and pecks at Darvish violently until my best friend flees to the safety of my beanbag chair.

"Hey!" Darvish cries. "That bird has problems!"

Despite Darvish's experience with animals, I do not think my practice pet likes him. Maybe it senses some character flaw I have not yet discovered.

Having claimed my bed as its own, the chicken nuzzles in next to me and does the chicken version of purring.

"Aw," says Darvish. "I think it likes you!"

If this were a dog, my heart would be melting. If this were a puppy, I would cherish this moment forever. But it is a chicken. So instead of having an emotional moment, I take advantage of its misplaced trust. I quickly lasso its neck with my makeshift leash and we take our first walk to PetPlanet.

Only this bird seems to resent being plucked from its roost on my bed. Either that, or chickens just don't like to walk. So we take more of a drag to PetPlanet.

My chicken clucks loudly the entire way. Perhaps it is excited.

Who can blame it? Being my gift AND getting to go to the store? This chicken is having a big day.

6

There is not much to do in Middling Falls. We have a library. A small zoo. A bowling alley. We are also the albino squirrel capital of the northwest, so that's a big deal if you are into really pale rodents.

Otherwise, this town is a wad of lint in the belly button of the modern world. Which means Buy-Buy Plaza is usually crowded.

Because of that, the parking lot is always under construction.

It stinks of fresh asphalt and sweaty construction workers.

And all manner of people hover on the sidewalk outside the stores begging for signatures and charitable donations.

Darvish's bookish demeanor makes him an easy mark. The poor guy has *sucker* written all over him.

The Pixie Scout girls attack first, hawking their baked goods. "'Scuse me, sir!" they say, assaulting my personal space bubble with their perkiness. "Wanna buy some Pixie Scout cookies? Only three dollars a box!"

"No thanks."

Darvish starts to slow down. "But, Rex, I LOVE Pixie Scout cookies! Especially the ones with the chocolate and coconut!"

See? He's a wounded gazelle among these predators, waiting to be devoured. I grab his shirt and keep walking.

A teenager waves a clipboard in our faces. He's wearing a tie and a big button that says PUPAE. "Join PUPAE, guys! The animals need you!"

"No thanks." Keep walking. That's the key.

"Donate to the Loyal Order of the Wombat!" screeches a guy in a fuzzy hat.

"No thanks."

"Get your tickets to the Firemen's Taco Tuesday!" yells a toothy fireman.

"REX!" yells Darvish. "TACOS!"

I pick up my pace. Luckily for him, he's got me for a friend. Otherwise his entire allowance would go to

Pixie Scout cookies, the Wombat Lodge, and firehouse tacos. It is good I am here to save him from himself.

We're almost to the door of PetPlanet. Glorious pet-centric respite awaits.

But suddenly . . . we see it.

At first, it looks like an arcade game from the eighties.

But I quickly see it's not a video game. It's an old-style carnival game.

And it's not from the eighties. It's much older. And much cooler.

There's a joystick and several buttons. But instead of a screen, there's a glass case that holds a life-size Grim Reaper.

His black hood rests on his bone-white skull. Skeletal hands stick out from the sleeves, with their palms open, beckoning us to play. Old-fashioned letters across the top display the name of the game: THE REAPER'S CURSE.

I turn to Darvish. "*This* is worth stopping for. How did something this cool wind up in Middling Falls?"

He looks skeptical. "I don't know. Looks weird. How do you play?"

"Who cares?" I say. "Look! It only costs twenty-five cents!"

I fish around in my pocket. Nothing.

"Loan me a quarter, Darvish."

"Loan?" he clarifies, rooting in his pocket. "You're going to pay me back?"

"Probably not," I confess.

He puts the quarter in my palm and I stick it into the coin slot.

We wait. Nothing happens.

"Aw, man," says Darvish. "You wasted a perfectly good quarter for nothing. It's busted."

"It's vintage," I say. "Give it a chance."

I bang on the front. Nothing.

I kick it. Nothing.

I grab the case and try to shake it into submission. The thing weighs a ton. It must be made of solid iron.

"Is it plugged in?" asks Darvish.

I look around the side of the case and see something disturbing. The power cord is plugged into the wall. But I had forgotten about my chicken.

It's pecking curiously at the plug. It's like watching a toddler shove a grape up its nose. You know you should stop it, but you kind of want to see what happens. I'm not saying I'm proud of these thoughts. I'm just being honest.

And then it happens.

The chicken pees. Right on the plug.

"Interesting fact," says Darvish. "Did you know chickens don't technically pee? Their pee mixes with their poop and it all comes out in kind of a combo pile. They don't pee or poop. They peep."

My friend has a knack for repulsive trivia. "Well, my chicken is doing a peep right on the electrical cord." This bird is not the brightest crayon in the box.

Sparks fly and there's a small series of zapping sounds. Darvish and I jump. But the chicken seems fine.

There's a hum from the game and it roars to life.

"I told you it just needed to warm up."

The Grim Reaper inside starts to move. He puts his bony hand near a small chute and my quarter falls into his palm. Behind him, a little sign spins into place:

PLAY AGAINST THE GRIM REAPER

WIN AND YOUR WISH IS GRANTED

LOSE AND SUFFER THE REAPER'S CURSE!

"Whoa!" cries Darvish in realization. "This is just like that old movie from the eighties."

"What movie?" I ask.

"You know," he persists. "The one with Tom Hanks."

"Never heard of him."

"He wishes to be tall," Darvish says. "Or grown. What was it called? *Tall*? *Large*?"

"No idea," I tell him. "Unlike you, I do not spend my time on ancient movies from a bygone era."

The Grim Reaper points to a little light-up sign on the front of the case:

DO YOU CHALLENGE THE REAPER'S CURSE?

"This is creepy," Darvish mutters. "My people don't like skeletons."

"What people are you talking about?" I ask. "People from Pakistan?"

"No," he says. "Scaredy-cats."

"Don't be a baby," I say, nudging him. "This is the coolest game I've ever seen." I reach out and tap the YES button.

"Well, be careful," says Darvish. "It didn't work out good for Tom Hanks."

Behind the Grim Reaper, a new sign lights up:

MAKE YOUR WISH

"What are you going to wish for?" asks Darvish.

"Easy," I say. I look at the Grim Reaper right in his glowing eyes. "I wish I had a real-live pet, instead of this chicken."

The Reaper in the case jerkily comes to life. It puts the quarter on the counter in front of it. Its skeleton fingers pull out three tin cups and place them in a row before me. The Reaper moves the third cup over the quarter.

FOLLOW THE COIN lights up.

The Grim Reaper begins to slide the cups around

the counter. It rearranges them. It figure-eights them. It swaps them around, always keeping my quarter hidden. I follow the cups with my eyes, tracking my quarter's movements. After several seconds and a few especially tricky switches, it stops. Another sign lights up:

FIND THE COIN

"Easy," I say.

"Dude, it's only supposed to look easy," says Darvish. "This is the Grim Reaper you're dealing with."

"This is a skeleton robot from 1935 I'm dealing with," I say. "I think I can handle him."

There are three buttons next to the joystick. They are labeled LEFT, MIDDLE, and RIGHT. I punch the MIDDLE button.

The Reaper reaches out with its hand and grasps the middle cup. It raises the cup to reveal . . .

. . . nothing. The quarter isn't there.

The Reaper's head rears back, lower jaw moving as a sinister laugh comes from the machine. It removes the cups from view. All the little signs turn off and the machine grows quiet, like it has reset to its starting position.

There's a little *"ding"* sound from the bottom of the machine. I look down. The Reaper's machine spits out a small card from a slot in the front.

YOU LOST!

YOUR WISH SHALL NOT BE GRANTED.

MY CURSE NOW LEAVES YOU THUS ENCHANTED.

A REAL-LIVE PET, THAT'S WHAT YOU'VE WISHED.

A PET YOU'LL GET, BUT THERE'S A TWIST!

FOR ANIMALS OF EVERY SIZE

WILL PASS AWAY, THEN OPEN EYES!

WHEN DEATH LEAVES QUESTIONS OF MYSTIQUE

THEIR SPIRITS LINGER, EYELIDS PEEK

TO FIND THEIR ANSWERS . . . YOU THEY'LL SEEK!

THIS IS THE ENDING OF MY VERSE

AND NOW, ENJOY THE REAPER'S CURSE.

"Well, that's weird and horrifyingly specific," I say. "Let's get my chicken supplies and get out of here."

"Oh my gosh, dude," Darvish says. His voice is suddenly choked and strained. He tugs on my sleeve. "I don't think that's going to be necessary."

I turn slowly around toward the parking lot. There, at the end of my rope, is the chicken.

Or what used to be the chicken. I can't believe what I'm seeing.

My chicken is dead. It's been squashed paper-thin by the steamroller that is repaving the asphalt.

I am stunned into silence.

I am aghast.

I am gobsmacked.

"I told you not to challenge the Reaper's Curse!" says Darvish. "I think I'm going to be sick!"

My poor chicken. It never had a chance. True, it was hardly a real pet. But despite its shortcomings, I would never wish this fate on it. This flat, squished fate.

For some reason, I think to check the time. And I realize that it has been one hour and fourteen minutes since I came into possession of the chicken. It's a new record for me. It's forty-seven minutes longer than Bub lasted.

I'm pretty sure I'm making progress on this whole responsibility thing.

I look down at the card in my hand. I turn it over. There's a picture of a skull on the front, shrouded in green mist. I could swear it's laughing.

Classic.

7

Oddly enough, my parents do not seem to think that I am making progress on this whole responsibility thing.

I'd rather not talk about the events of the rest of the day. Events that involved me having to explain how I allowed my brand-new chicken to be crushed into a poultry pancake.

Events that involved my mom shaking her head and rubbing her eyes.

Events that involved my dad uttering phrases like "never getting a dog," and "go to your room," and "where is my anti-anxiety medication?"

Events that involved Darvish throwing up. (That

kid has a weak stomach when it comes to flattened animals.)

Please stop pestering me for details. I said I don't want to talk about it.

What I will talk about is how I'm lying in my bed. Which, right now, is about the furthest place from getting a chocolate Lab as anywhere on earth. I'm still dazed from the way this rotten day has gone from bad to worse.

I know it's selfish to feel bad for myself. I should feel bad for the chicken. And I do. Proper pet or not, nobody deserves to perish at the mercy of a rampaging steamroller.

I pull the Grim Reaper's card out of my pocket. It has to be just a coincidence that my chicken dies a gruesome death just seconds after I lose a bet with Death. But it's an awfully weird one.

I shiver. My room is suddenly freezing. My dad must be punishing me further by turning the heat down.

That's when I hear a low scraping sound. It's a kind of a shuffling noise, like a sack of Puppy Chow being dragged across the floor. I sit up and look around the room, but of course there's nothing there. I know I'm alone.

A chill runs up my spine. I can practically see my breath forming in the dimness before me, that's how frosty it's gotten. The room has started to darken as twilight creeps in through the window blinds. But I don't get up to turn on the light. I just lie there. I'm in mourning. For my birthday. For my dignity. Oh yeah, and for my chicken.

I shiver again. The poor thing. It didn't even have a name, for crying out loud.

"I didn't even have a name, for crying out loud," somebody says.

Only, there are currently no other somebodies in my room.

I see a flash of movement out of the corner of my eye. I turn my head, but there's nothing there.

Which rates about a six on the Spooky Meter. The hairs on my arms stand on end.

I look at my bedroom door. Closed.

I look at my closet. Open and empty.

I look at the foot of my bed.

A dead chicken looks back at me.

My blood runs cold. I scramble back, knocking my lamp off the table.

It hovers over the end of my bed, this farmyard phantom. It is pale. And squashed. A ghostly fritter of its former self. It gazes at me with a cold, dead stare. Sickly green vapors rise from the fowl vision before me.

I try to talk, but my breath catches. I clear my throat, take a ragged, shaky breath, and attempt to communicate with the apparition before me.

"What are you?" I whisper.

But I know what it is. There is only one possible explanation.

It is the ghost of my dead chicken. A vengeful spirit. A specter. Tortilla-flat and ready to exact its revenge upon me.

Which rates about a nine on the Spooky Meter. Which should now be referred to as the Horrifically Hideous Spooky Meter of Doom.

Unless the Horrifically Hideous Spooky Meter of Doom is a scale of one through five. In which case, it rates a five.

Unless the Horrifically Hideous Spooky Meter of Doom is like the DEFCON scale, where one is high and five is low. In which case, what genius came up with that idea? Like people have time to perform a mathematical conversion when they are in the presence of something horrifically hideous.

I shiver again.

Then its beak opens. I tremble in anticipation of what it will say. What possible otherworldly condemnation can it utter at me for allowing its recent and undignified demise?

Two words issue forth from its pitch-black squawk-box of horror.

"Hiya, bestie!"

8

'm having a conversation with my dead chicken. A weird, weird conversation.

"I'm sorry. What did you say?"

"I said, 'Hiya, bestie!'" the chicken says.

I look around the room for garlic or a wooden stake. Nothing. My dad's been tidying my room again without asking. I hold my fingers in a cross before me. "What do you want, spirit?" I ask it.

"I dunno."

"What are you doing here, phantom?" I demand.

"I dunno."

"How come you can talk, apparition?"

"I've always talked. I have a lot to say."

"Fine. How come I can understand you?"

"I dunno."

This chicken is no more helpful in death than it was in life.

"Don't you have somewhere else you should be?" I ask.

"Like where?"

"Like moving toward the bright light?" I suggest.

"I did see a bright light!" cries the chicken. "Earlier. Shining at me through a tunnel."

"I think you were supposed to go toward it," I say.

"I thought it was another steamroller," says the chicken. "Did you see that steamroller? It almost hit me."

"It did hit you."

"Okay."

"Why didn't you go toward the bright light?" I ask.

"I started to. But something stopped me. I felt like I was supposed to stay here. With you."

"Why?" I ask.

"I dunno, bestie," it says. "For some reason, I felt like maybe you needed me."

"I don't. And quit calling me *bestie*."

"Should I call you BFF?"

"No."

"Should I call you homie?"

"No."

"Should I call you bro? Chief? Amigo? El Jefe?"

"Just call me Rex."

There's a long silence.

"REEEEEEEEEEEEEEX!" Its ghostly howl sends me diving under the blankets.

"What?!" I screech.

"Nothing," it says. "I was just trying it out. It's not much of a best buddy nickname, but it's a start. So how about a name for me, Rex?"

First, I am having a conversation with a dead bird. Second, he's a real comedian. Third, he apparently feels bad that he is nameless. Things are getting weirder by the minute. And not in an awesome way.

"Why would a dead chicken need a name?" I ask.

"So you know what to call me, of course. Duh!"

"Are we really going to be talking often enough for that to be a problem?"

"Oh, I'll be here for a while," he says. "As long as you need me."

"But I don't need you now," I say.

"Okay."

I'm getting nowhere with this. "Fine. How about Flat Chicken?"

He thinks about it for a second. "Nope. That's a description, not a name."

"Nugget?" I suggest.

"No."

"How about Roadkill?"

"Hmm." He considers. "That makes me sound dangerous. Like I have a past."

"You do have a past," I remind him. "You are actual roadkill."

"No," he decides. "It's not quite right."

"Drumstick?" I suggest.

He walks around the bed, thinking it over. When he turns sideways, I can barely see him. He's paper-thin. That steamroller really did a number on him.

"I like it!" he says. "Drumstick it is!"

The bird sits down on my comforter. His green otherworldly vapor pools around him like a puddle of toxic waste. He scratches his beak with his foot. "You should probably get some sleep," he says.

"Why?" I ask.

"You're going to need your rest. I think your life is about to get cuckoo."

"What's that supposed to mean?"

"I dunno."

I think my life may already be cuckoo. But he's right. The events of this day have exhausted me.

I lie down. If this chicken is here to be my spirit guide, I'm pretty sure he's doing it wrong. I think I got a trainee by mistake.

"Are you just going to sit there while I sleep?" I ask. "Not that that's creepy."

It is creepy.

"I'm fine, buddy old pal," he clucks. "I'm just happy we're back together again."

I roll over, pull my covers up to my face. The room is freezing. I try not to think about the fact that there's a dead barnyard bird sitting on the edge of my bed.

Darvish is never going to believe it. And that kid believes everything.

9

Darvish doesn't believe it. And that kid believes everything.

"I don't believe it," Darvish whispers. "You must think I'm a real dummy."

He is whispering because Ms. Yardley is currently talking about fractions.

My teacher is a well-educated employee of the state. However, she has a troubling obsession with fractions. I don't think she believes in anything being whole. All she can talk about are glasses of water that are only one-fifth full, and pizza split into eighths and two-tenths of a sandwich. You'd think it would be a sad way to go through life, never getting a whole sandwich to yourself, but she seems to adore the idea of partial portions.

However, I am not currently listening to her fraction-focused spiel because I have more pressing business. Like convincing my best friend that I am being visited by the ghost of chickens past.

"We've established you don't believe me," I whisper back. "But it's true."

"Like Poopsylvania true?" he asks.

He is not playing fair, throwing my past transgressions in my face.

"That was a whimsical exaggeration," I clarify. "A flight of fancy to keep your life interesting."

"My life is plenty interesting."

"Mine too," whispers Sami Mulpepper from across the row. "For example, I find fractions very interesting."

I shake my head sadly. These people need to learn the joys of whole numbers.

"But right now, I can't hear anything about fractions because someone is chatting to Darvish."

I turn to her. "Sami, please quit distracting me."

"Distracting *you*?" she huffs.

"Yes," I say. "I am dealing with otherworldly issues from the great beyond. This is no time for frivolous math equations or random discussions with tawny-haired classmates."

Sami smiles. "Did you just call my hair tawny?"

"What?" I say. "Don't be ludicrous."

"Mm-hm," she says, grinning mysteriously. "Just pipe down, okay?" She turns back around.

"*Tawny* has lots of meanings, you know," I whisper at her. She ignores me.

"She's finally snapped," I tell Darvish. "I knew this day would come."

"Mm-hm," he says, grinning mysteriously.

I roll my eyes and return to the matter at hand. "Look, Darvish. You are my best friend. My one true compadre. If I tell you I'm being plagued by phantom poultry, you are required to believe me."

"We can talk about this later," whispers Darvish. "You're going to get me in trouble."

"Strange happenings are happening," I hiss. "They require immediate attention, no matter what certain Mulpeppers have to say on the subject."

Sami Mulpepper's love of fractions and shaky hold on reality are not the most troubling things about her at the moment. Her interruption has caused me to lower my guard. Which has allowed Ms. Yardley to sneak up on us like the wily predator that she is.

"Rex and Darvish," says Ms. Yardley. "Do I have your full attention?"

"Yes," says Darvish.

"Only about three-eighths," I admit.

10

Adults say they want honesty. It is a lie and a sham. And now I am being forced to make posters.

Convincing your best friend that supernatural happenings are afoot is difficult under the best of conditions.

It is doubly so when the two of you are elbow-deep in glitter and smelly markers.

In a couple weeks, our school will have a dance. It is called the Evening of Enchantment Dance. Much of our student body is quite excited about this vulgar shindig. Not me.

I have never been to a dance, but, as I understand, it works like this: On the night in question, students will dress in garish finery. They will gather in the school gymnasium for refreshment and loud DJ music. And they will cut a rug. Bust a move. Boogie down.

I think not.

However, as punishment for talking in class, Ms. Yardley has assigned Darvish and me to create glitzy posters advertising this sordid affair.

This is called child abuse. It is also called recess detention. Either way, it is probably illegal. I'm starting to think that Ms. Yardley has no regard for the laws of man or nature.

Thankfully, Ms. Yardley considers recess her "prep" time. Which means she is currently in the teacher's lounge eating chocolate cake and gossiping with the school nurse. This leaves Darvish and me free to discuss the important issues of the day.

"So, you're telling me that a dead chicken slept in your room?" Darvish clarifies.

"Not *a* dead chicken," I say. "*The* dead chicken. I don't know if he slept. And I think he might be a rooster. He definitely had a guy's voice."

"Did it have a big comb?" he asks.

"I don't think so," I reply. "But it needed one. Its feathers were a mess."

"Not that kind of comb," says Darvish, shaking his head. "The red flap on the top of a rooster's head is called a comb. A rooster's comb is bigger than a hen's comb."

"Quit saying *comb*," I tell him. "You know way too much about farm animals."

He sprinkles glitter across his poster. "The chicken you got for your birthday was a rooster. It had a big comb."

"Well, then the dead chicken in my bedroom last night was a rooster. Because it was the same one."

I have glitter and confetti stuck to every exposed surface of my skin. It is making me itch. I think I'm developing an allergic reaction. Or mono. Or whooping crane. My diagnosis is unclear.

"You're telling me that the ghost of your dead rooster is talking to you?" Darvish asks.

"Yes!" I say. "Though he didn't seem to think he was a ghost. And he wasn't see-through. But there were green vapors flowing around him. I'm pretty sure it was some type of firm-bodied apparition."

"So, you're being haunted by your rooster?"

"Well, anything sounds ridiculous if you say it with that attitude," I point out.

"Did he say *Boo*?"

"No."

"Did he rattle chains?"

"No," I say. Darvish can be really sarcastic when he wants to be. I usually consider sarcasm an asset. However, a little sincerity would be helpful right now. "He just hung out in my room. We chatted."

"So where is this phantom chicken?" he asks, looking around the art room. "I don't see any ghost birds around here."

I shrug. "I don't know. He was gone when I woke up this morning."

"That's convenient," he says, pulling out a pink marker and brandishing it at a fresh piece of poster board. "It was probably just a dream. Guilt can do strange things to your REM sleep cycles, dude."

"First, I am not guilty of anything," I clarify. "Second, I did not dream it." I sigh and shake my head. I'm getting nowhere. If you ask me, Darvish picked a rotten time to stop being gullible.

I snatch up a wrinkled poster board from a dusty pile in the corner. "Gross. This thing has a dead bug stuck to it." I flick the bug to the floor.

"Is it talking to you?"

"What? No!"

"Why not?" he asks sarcastically, gluing down a large sparkly star. "I thought dead animals were talking to you."

"They are! Well, a chicken is!" I throw my glue bottle to the table. "I don't know how this works!" I take a deep cleansing breath. "Look, I know this sounds made up. But I'm telling you the truth. I'm seeing ghosts."

"Uh-huh."

"I mean it."

"Uh-huh."

I grab Darvish by the shirt and look him square in the eye. "I so solemnly swear. Cross my heart and hope to never ever own a chocolate Labrador of my very own."

This stops Darvish in his tracks. Glue drips from his bottle onto his shoes. But he fails to notice. "Wait a minute. You're serious."

It's the biggest, most serious swear I can make, and only a best friend would know it.

"Dead serious," I say. "Dead animals are talking to me."

"Whoa."

"So, you believe me?"

"I'm required to believe you. You made the chocolate Lab swear. It's the biggest, most serious swear you can make."

I breathe a sigh of relief. Thank goodness for the chocolate Lab swear.

11

Undead barnyard birds. Fractions. Recess detention. And I now have glitter on my arms that will not wash off.

The events of the last twenty-four hours have been troubling, to say the least. I blame at least three of the four on my teacher. Among these relentless trials, there is one thing that has driven me back from the precipice of total and debilitating madness.

Darvish is back to believing everything I tell him.

It is a welcome development. When you are under siege by fiends from the underworld, it's nice to have somebody to chat with about it.

We are in my room, where Darvish is eating a

baggie-ful of leftover pizza crusts. He has decided to deploy the "Scientific Method" in our situation.

I fail to see how this helps us. "Yes, I understand," I tell him. "Rain evaporates and turns into clouds. What does that have to do with ghost chickens?"

"That's the Water Cycle," Darvish says. "I'm talking about the Scientific Method. We learned it in school."

"It's possible I was not paying attention on that day." It's been known to happen. It's not technically my fault. Clever and wily though she is, my teacher has not honed the fine art of giving your audience what they want. But if it leads to a solution, I will let Darvish continue down this path. Though his Parmesan-scented smacking is doing nothing for my frayed nerves.

He taps his chin thoughtfully. "Your hypothesis is that there is a ghostly chicken appearing to you that nobody else can see or hear," Darvish states for the record.

"I don't have a hypothesis," I clarify, scratching my arm. "I may have a glitter allergy."

"Right. So, the chicken is here right now?" he asks.

"Yes, he's sitting right next to me," I say.

"Two best buddies," Drumstick says. "Sitting together!"

"You can't see him?" I ask Darvish. "He's right here."

"I don't see anything," he says. "Except you. And an empty beanbag chair."

"Why is he here?" asks Drumstick. "I thought this was just going to be us."

"He's here to help us figure this out," I tell him.

"Ah." My chicken points at Darvish. "And why is he dressed like that?"

I look at Darvish's polo shirt and khaki pants. I shrug. "He always dresses like a golf instructor. I think he even irons his shoes. I understand that it is disconcerting at first. You get used to it."

Darvish gives me a stern look. "This is my school uniform and you know it."

"Our school doesn't have uniforms, Darvish," I remind him.

"Well, they should."

Drumstick sighs. "It reminds me of a pigeon I once knew. Gosh, what a great bird. He had a little paper bag he wore as a sweater vest."

"Uniforms promote an environment of academic excellence and rigorous learning," Darvish says. He brushes imaginary dirt indignantly from his pants. "Besides, everyone looks good in khaki."

"Darvish, you said you'd help me. Quit primping and focus!" I point at Drumstick. "Look closely, now. You can't see his swirly green ghost-mist?"

"Nope."

Drumstick looks up at me. "I'm not sure this kid is the sharpest beak in the henhouse. Maybe we'd be better off without him."

I turn to Darvish. "You didn't hear that?"

"Hear what?"

"He just slammed you," I explain. "It was witty and cutting. Especially for poultry."

"The dead chicken is insulting me?"

Drumstick tugs on my sleeve. "And he's not using my name."

"He doesn't like you calling him 'the dead chicken,'" I explain. "His name is Drumstick."

"I'm not calling him that," says Darvish.

"Then we shan't be talking," says Drumstick with a *humph*.

"Let's conduct a methodical and objective experiment," suggests Darvish.

"In the name of the Water Cycle?" I ask.

"The Scientific Method."

"If you say so."

Darvish reaches into his pocket and pulls out his cell phone. "Let's try to take a picture of him. Maybe the lens can pick up more than the naked eye."

Drumstick tugs on my sleeve. "He said *naked*." He giggles into his wing.

This bird is really growing on me.

Nakedness aside, it's a good idea. If we capture

photographic evidence, not only will Darvish be able to see Drumstick and assuage his scientific curiosity, but I'll be able to retire while I'm still in my prime. I hear people pay premium cash for evidence of life after death. Once again, I've taken a simply good idea of Darvish's and transformed it into a brilliant and lucrative plan.

Except it doesn't work.

"No good," says Darvish, showing me the screen.

"I changed my mind. This guy is nothing like my pigeon friend," Drumstick says, pointing at Darvish. "And he's kind of bringing down our special hangout time."

Darvish zooms in on the picture. "It's just you and an empty beanbag chair. He's not there."

"I am here!" Drumstick is starting to get worked up. It's not a good color on him.

Darvish shakes his head. "I hate to suggest it. But is it possible you're just imagining things?"

"Imagining things?" Drumstick cries angrily. "Is it possible to imagine the love blossoming in your heart for your newest boon companion? Is it possible to imagine the unique once-in-a-century bond you share with your soul mate? I think not!"

Drumstick storms up to Darvish. "He's just doing it wrong! Let me see that thing!"

The chicken reaches out for the cell phone, but his

flat flippers are no good at grabbing and he just swats the phone to the floor.

"Whoa!" Darvish goes pale. "Did you see that?"

"I know." I nod. "He's terrible at grabbing stuff. It's the flattened wings. Plus, you're upsetting him."

And then it hits me. "WAIT! YOU SAW THAT?"

Darvish's hands are shaking. "My phone was just knocked right out of my hand! I felt something hit it!" He bends down and picks it up off the floor.

I turn to Drumstick. "How did you do that?"

"Do what?"

"You just knocked Darvish's phone out of his hand!"

"Okay."

"How did you do it?"

The chicken shrugs. "I dunno. I just got excited. I wanted to show this guy how to make it work." He reaches out, but his wing passes right through the phone. He shrugs again and nuzzles into the crook of my arm.

"How did he do it?" asks Darvish.

"Don't know," I tell him. "He got excited."

"Interesting," says Darvish. "Emotional kinetic discharge. I've read about this."

"English, Darvish."

He's pacing around mumbling to himself. It's nice to see him taking an interest.

"He can only touch stuff when he's excited or upset," he says. "Have him do it again."

"Nope," mutters Drumstick. "Not while he's here."

"He doesn't want to," I say, shaking my head at Darvish. "I don't think he likes you."

"Doesn't like me?" Darvish exclaims. "What's not to like? I'm incredibly likable!"

My best friend's likability aside, his scientific approach has borne fruit. Because we now know I'm not imagining things.

Which means my deepest darkest fear has come true. Next to falling into a pit of snakes. And global takeover by evil robots. And paper cuts. These are the things that haunt my nightmares.

My fourth deepest darkest fear has come true.

I have been cursed by a rogue carnival game. Just me. Since it was Darvish's quarter, I had really hoped we would be in this together. That would only be fair, right?

But no. Clearly, Darvish cannot see the dead. I'm all alone.

"I guess it's official," I say. "I've got the Reaper's Curse."

"I warned you to leave that game alone," Darvish says. "You should have listened to the wisdom of my people."

"We're talking about the fraidy-cats again?"

"It's scaredy-cats," he corrects me. "Don't mock us, dude. Our lore is rich with stories about avoiding skeletons, zombies, rusty nails, plastic dry-cleaner bags, and pretty much everything else that's creepy or slightly dangerous. How do you think we've survived as a people for so long?"

Darvish pauses for a minute and chomps thoughtfully on a pizza crust. "So, you're being haunted by your dead chicken." He taps his chin and looks at me. "I guess that only leaves one query unanswered."

"Why you eat such weird snacks?" I ask.

"No."

"What happened to the rest of your pizza?"

"Nope."

"Where did I get such a stylish beanbag chair?"

"No."

"You've brought it up several times. I know you like it."

"I do," he says, eyeing the chair jealously. "But that's not what we should be worrying about."

"What then?"

"What's the next ghost that's going to come for you?"

This is one query I wish we hadn't asked. Now I have a glitter allergy *and* acute anxiety syndrome.

This whole Scientific Method thing is a real downer. I think I prefer the Water Cycle.

12

Grown-ups get so confused about what's really important.

Here I am, grappling with the mysteries of the universe.

Here I am, unraveling the great veil that separates life and death.

Here I am, in an arm-wrestling match with the Grim Reaper himself.

And all Ms. Yardley wants to talk about is research reports. It is an upsetting situation.

"Your research must be thorough," she says, roaming the room like a fraction-loving jaguar. "Dynamic delivery is a great thing, but it must be supported by facts! Half of your grade will be on presentation, but the other fifty percent will be on your research."

"Yes!" cheers Sami Mulpepper. "Oral reports!"

An oral report in front of the class. While I'm stressing over the supernatural. It is a slap in the face of the vast and unfathomable cosmos.

"I'm excited too, Sami," says Ms. Yardley. "We will do four presentations per day starting next week. So be thinking about your topics! You can sign up for presentation time slots on the door later this week."

"Yay!" cheers Drumstick. "Oral reports!" He turns to me. "Rexxie, do we like oral reports?"

"We do not," I whisper.

"Boo!" cries Drumstick. "Oral reports!"

Thankfully, I have people in my life that appreciate my predicament. And one of those people is a dead chicken. That's right. He's started coming to school with me.

"Don't call me Rexxie," I whisper.

"It's okay," says Drumstick. "It's like a best-buddy nickname."

"You're not my best buddy."

"I'm not? Who is?"

"Darvish."

"That kid who was intruding on our you-and-me time yesterday?"

"Yes."

"I never liked that kid," says Drumstick. "I pecked him from the moment I met him."

"Well, he's my best friend."

"Oh. Okay. That's cool. Then it's like a second-best-buddy nickname."

"All right."

"Do you have a best-buddy handshake with that kid?"

"No."

"Good. I think we should come up with a second-best-buddy secret handshake that only you and I know."

"Maybe later."

"That's cool. That's cool."

Ms. Yardley locks on to me with her heat-seeking hawk eyes. "Rex, you seem awfully chatty back there. Do you have a question or comment about our oral reports?"

It's like she is reading my mind. "As a matter of fact, I do. It seems to me that an oral report is kind of a waste of time."

Ms. Yardley sighs. "This assignment is a valuable study on the power of research, Rex."

"I'm a man of action," I tell her. "I prefer to experience life rather than read about it."

"Well, if you'd like a good grade on your report, you'll be a man of research."

"Perhaps I can simply tell the class about something that I've experienced in my everyday life," I suggest. "You can rest assured they'll be mesmerized."

"No, Rex," she says. "You may not."

I stand up on my desk to make myself appear bigger. It is a technique that many dog breeds employ to establish dominance. "I didn't want to do this, but I'll need to take your Teacher Identification Number."

She goes slack-jawed. This technique can have that effect. "I'm sorry. My what?"

"Your TIN," I state. "I feel that you may be stifling my creative expression. I'll need to report this incident to the appropriate authorities."

My classmates wear stunned expressions. They are clearly hypnotized by my charisma. Plus, watching me haggle with our teacher is probably more fun than discussing research reports. So they say nothing.

"Please sit down, Rex," she says through gritted teeth.

I sense her anger is rising. For her sake, I do not want a scene. I sit.

My teacher takes a deep breath and continues to address the class. "To help us appreciate the power of research, we will be studying current events over the next several weeks. You were told that you could bring a current event from the newspaper or the Internet to read to the class for extra credit." She takes her seat. "Who has one they would like to share?"

Edwin Willoughby reads an article about a new video-game release.

Holly Creskin shares an article about a fire at the zoo. Apparently, a rare Sumatran rhinoceros was killed in the blaze. It is a tragic affair.

Sami Mulpepper quotes some article from the *Middling Falls Daily Spew.*

But my mind is wandering. Partly because it is difficult to stay invested in events, whether current or otherwise, that are not directly about me.

Partly because I do not care what Sami Mulpepper has to say in general. Despite her charismatic delivery.

And partly because Edwin's video-game article has given me a flash of inspiration.

"*The Reaper's Curse,*" I hiss to Darvish. "That's it."

"What's it?" asks Darvish.

"What's it?" asks Drumstick.

"We'll go back to the game," I whisper. "I'll beat the game and wish to be uncursed."

Drumstick shakes his steamrolled head nervously. "Ooh, I'm not sure that's such a good idea. I died last time I went near that game. I don't want that to happen again."

Darvish also looks dubious. He is widely known for his dubiousness. It is his third most common facial expression, right behind quizzical and hungry. "I don't know, Rex. What if you lose again and get double cursed?"

"You underestimate my cunning."

"Well, you're right about that," he confirms.

"My cunning is its own kind of curse," I remind him.

"If you say so."

"But it's a valid point," I concede. "New plan. You can play and wish me uncursed. That way, if you lose, you'll only get cursed once."

"No way, dude." He shakes his head firmly. "No way."

I'm not sure who is the bigger chicken. Darvish or Drumstick.

"Fine," I say. "I'll do it myself."

"This is going to end badly," Darvish mumbles.

"Clear your calendars," I tell my two compatriots.

"I don't use a calendar," says Darvish. "I'm a kid. I mostly just play and do homework in an unscheduled fashion."

"Nothing to clear, pal!" says Drumstick. "I have us scheduled for a tickle-fight tomorrow afternoon. Other than that, I'm wide open for the rest of eternity. I mostly just follow you around."

"Clear them anyway," I say. I lean back in my chair confidently and smile. "After school today, we're going back to beat the Reaper's Curse."

Apparently, I lean a little too confidently. My chair tips backward and I clatter confidently to the floor.

Ms. Yardley looks at me. Then she thumps her head slowly and repeatedly against her desk.

"I was wrong to underestimate your cunning," says Darvish. "We clearly have nothing to worry about."

13

I am surrounded by skeptics.

But I have the boldness that comes with surviving a near-death experience at the hands of faulty school furniture. The stride of a mature and responsible person taking control of his destiny. The doubters trail me, adrift in the wake of my moxie.

"Slow down, buddy," complains Drumstick. "Your confident strides are making me tired. I have little legs."

"Why are you even here?" I ask him.

"You asked me to come!" says Darvish. "You called me your backup!"

"I'm not talking to you," I clarify. "I'm talking to the chicken."

"I can't hear the chicken!" says Darvish.

That's right. This is going to take some getting used to. "Sorry. I forgot."

"I want to see what happens," says Drumstick. "Plus, I love you!"

I have to confess, this bird is starting to melt through my hard candy shell. Soon, my nougaty soft center will be exposed to the heartbreaks and disappointments of this cruel world. I'm not sure how I feel about that. Once the Reaper's Curse is lifted, he will be on his way. Perhaps that is for the best. I stiffen my resolve and march on.

The air smells of purpose and strawberries. Darvish is eating the strawberries. I do not know where he got them. All I know is that strawberries are a lighthearted fruit. Far too lighthearted for the serious mission at hand. He should be snacking on kiwi, if anything. That's a fruit that says *I mean business*.

All the usual suspects are hanging out at Buy-Buy Plaza.

"Wanna buy Pixie Scout cookies, mister?" squawk the Pixie Scout girls.

"Hey, sign up for PUPAE, fellas," says the PUPAE guy, waving his clipboard. "Only fifty-nine ninety-nine! We're one hundred members strong! Our animal rights campaign is getting really aggressive."

"Give to our clothes drive!" screeches the old guy from the Loyal Order of the Wombat.

"Tickets for Taco Tuesday!" shrieks the fireman.

I ignore them all. I'm a man with a plan.

My plan is simple, but brilliant. I will challenge the Grim Reaper at his own game. I will wish to be freed from his curse. I will emerge triumphant. It's the perfect strategy. Nothing can go wrong.

But as we approach the metal-and-glass box of the game console, I realize I have been foiled by forces larger than myself. The one diabolical snag that nobody, and I mean nobody, could have possibly predicted.

There's an OUT OF ORDER sign on *The Reaper's Curse.*

Well played, Grim Reaper. Well played.

But I am not so easily daunted. I toss the sign to the ground and stare at the skeletal visage of my adversary. He stares back from within his glass case, empty eye sockets mocking me.

I'm glad I brought backup. I turn to Darvish. "Loan me another quarter."

"Another one?" He reaches into his pocket. "You need to start carrying cash."

I pop the quarter into the coin slot. Nothing happens.

I kick the game cabinet. Nothing.

I rock it back and forth. It barely budges. Nothing lights up. Nothing moves. The Reaper just sits there defiantly.

Drumstick tugs on my pants leg. "I think some-body needs to go to the bathroom on it," he suggests. "That's what worked before."

I am loath to admit it, but, of course, the bird is right. I turn to my best friend. "Darvish, being my backup is a two-pronged position. Financing our mission is only the first prong."

"What's the second prong?"

"You're going to have to pee on the plug."

"What???" He screeches higher than I realized was possible. "Forget it!"

"Pee is the only way to summon the magic, Darvish."

"I told you, chickens don't pee," he cries. "It's basic science. Birds poop and pee together. They peep!"

"Well," I reason, "unless you have peeping skills I don't know about, we're going to have to make do with you peeing on it."

"Make the chicken do it!" he says. "That's what worked last time!"

I look to Drumstick, but he just shrugs. "I haven't gone since I died," he says. "I don't think dead things have to go to the bathroom."

I grab Darvish by the shoulders. "Ghosts don't pee, Darvish. It's got to be you."

"Come on!"

"Do you want me to be cursed forever?"

Darvish sulks. "No."

"Do you want me to be haunted to the end of my days?"

Darvish sighs. "No."

"Please, Darvish. You're my best friend. Can you think of anyone else more qualified to take a leak on an electrical cord in my time of need?"

Darvish places his bag of strawberries on the ground. "I guess not."

He looks around to ensure there are no bystanders to witness his shame. "If this gets out, I'm never getting into the college of my choice. These things haunt your transcript forever." My best friend sidles up to the cord and makes the ultimate sacrifice.

"Is it working?" he yells.

I push buttons. I jiggle the joystick. I kick the game again.

Nothing.

"Nothing is happening," I tell Darvish. "Pee harder."

"I'm peeing as hard as I can!" he cries.

"Nothing."

"What?" he yells. "Are you telling me that I'm urinating in public for nothing?"

"It's not technically my fault, Darvish. Blame the Reaper."

The Grim Reaper is playing hard to get. It's a classic

move. This robotic replica of Death is shrewder than I have given him credit for.

And that's when it happens.

"Oh my gosh. That is so gross." A voice startles me.

I freeze in terror. A chill ripples through me. It's the fuzz. The po-po. The long arm of the law. We're caught with our pants down. Actually, nobody's pants are down. Only Darvish's zipper.

"Tell your friend to stop peeing in public," the voice cries. "Show some respect for yourself! Sheesh!"

I turn toward the voice.

But it's not the fuzz. It's not the po-po. It's not the long arm of the law.

It's a rhinoceros.

A charred rhinoceros.

A blackened rhinoceros.

A burnt-to-a-crisp rhinoceros.

This is one dead rhino. Green ghost-goo pools at its feet. And its dead eyes are staring right at me.

"AAAGGGHHH!" I screech in terror. I stumble backward. With catlike reflexes, I try to catch myself. But this sidewalk must be faulty, because I slam into the pavement, falling face-first into a bag of strawberries.

The most lighthearted of all the fruits.

14

Despite all our advancements as a civilization, many facts about the natural world remain shrouded in secrecy.

For example, rhinos have absolutely no regard for the amount of soot that they track into other people's homes.

I know this because I have a dead rhino in my bedroom right now. Also, the rhino looks like a giant burnt Tater Tot.

Upon seeing the dead rhino at Buy-Buy Plaza, I decided to adopt a new and inspired strategy. I ran away. Fast. Like, scared-little-bunny-rabbit fast.

This perfectly formed strategy was foiled by forces beyond my comprehension. A maneuver so devious that nobody, and I mean nobody, could have predicted it.

The rhino was simply waiting in my bedroom when we arrived. Diabolical.

"Why is it so cold in here?" asks Darvish. "I can almost see my breath."

Darvish is also in my room. He sits and pants heavily. Our recent sprint has winded him.

"It always gets cold when they first appear," I say. I resist the urge to shiver. I refuse to give this rhino the satisfaction.

"And what's that black stuff all over your carpet?" asks Darvish.

"Those are ashes," I explain. "From the charbroiled rhino."

"Whoa. Ghost soot." He bends down to examine it. "He's in here right now? You're talking to a dead rhino right now?"

"Did he just call me a he?" says the rhino. "Wow. Just wow."

"What's the problem?" I ask the rhino.

"Hello? I'm a girl-rhino. Obviously." She snaps her girl-rhino fingers at Darvish.

"He's a she," I tell Darvish. "And yes. She is standing right there." I point at the rhino. "Tapping her foot."

"You better believe I'm tapping my foot," says the

rhino. "I'm telling you, that fire was no accident." She flounces heavily into my beanbag chair.

Great. Now that has to be washed, too.

"She's going on about some fire," I tell Darvish. Drumstick flutters up to perch by my side.

"Fire?" asks Darvish. He grabs me and shakes. "Holly Creskin!"

"Focus, man," I say. "This is no time to be daydreaming about girls."

"No!" he cries. "Holly read a story in current events today."

"I wasn't really listening," I say. "I have no interest in the babblings of a double cat owner who dislikes animals."

He slaps his forehead in frustration. Clearly, he feels similarly about Holly Creskin. "Her article was about a rhino at the zoo. A rhino that was killed in a fire!"

"Oh, yeah!" I say. The pieces are all coming together. "So, you're saying . . ."

"Yes!" cries Darvish.

". . . that the burnt rhino that's in my room right now . . ."

"Yes!" exclaims Darvish.

". . . probably knows the rhino that was killed in the fire!"

"No!" cries Darvish. "I'm saying she IS the rhino that was killed in the fire."

"If that's true, why would Tater Tot be here?" I ask.

"Who's Tater Tot?"

"It's what I'm calling her now." I turn to Tater Tot. "Why are you here?"

"Because you can hear me. Duh," she says. "I just knew you could. Don't know how. Don't know why. But I've got unfinished business and I need somebody who can listen. And that's you."

"Unfinished business?" I ask. "What am I supposed to do?"

"Something!" she yells. "Look, I heard somebody in my cage before the fire started. Next thing I know, I'm the only crispified citizen of Blazeytown. Don't you care that there's a rhino killer on the loose? Sheesh!"

"Sure, I guess I care about rhino killers," I say. "But you're dead now! Can't you just move on to rhino heaven and leave me alone?"

"Yeah!" squawks Drumstick. "Move on to rhino heaven!"

"You too!" I shout at him.

The chicken looks hurt. "Why would I move on to rhino heaven? I'm a chicken. If I move on to anywhere, shouldn't it be chicken heaven?"

"Whatever!" I say. "Why involve me in any of this?"

Darvish stands up and starts pacing. The kid paces when he gets excited. It is a nervous habit.

"The rhino wants something, doesn't she?" asks Darvish.

"She says the fire wasn't an accident," I tell Darvish. "Like I'm supposed to do something about it."

"I knew it. There's a reason they're coming to you."

"Yeah," I say. "Because they're annoying!"

"Don't you see?" he says. "She needs something from you." His pacing has picked up speed. "I've been giving this some thought. Remember what the curse said:

Animals of every size
Will pass away, then open eyes!
When death leaves questions of mystique
Their spirits linger, eyelids peek
To find their answers . . . YOU they'll seek!"

I grab the Grim Reaper card from my dresser. He's right. Word for word. Darvish really needs to get some hobbies. "How in the world did you remember that?"

"It's called reading."

"It's called strange," I say. "Seek help."

"Seek help," repeats Darvish. "That's exactly what they're doing! Seeking your help! I think you're supposed to help them."

"Help them do what?"

"Right some wrong. They're still tethered to this world."

"Yeah!" the rhino chimes in. "I'm tethered!"

"They need your help to finish something important before they can move on."

"You should listen to your little buddy," says Tater Tot. "Come on. Help me out. Just this last piece of unfinished business. Then I'll get out of your hair."

"Drumstick died without a name," Darvish says. "The rhino was murdered. They're coming to you because they need something. They need you to help them."

"But I gave the chicken a name," I say. "Why is he still here?"

"I don't know. Maybe he's here to help you. Maybe he's too dumb to know he's dead. Maybe he just really likes you."

Drumstick nods. "Those are all excellent theories. Ooh, look! A chocolate chip!" He starts pecking at the folds of my bedsheets.

Give me a big fat break. It's not my fault somebody put a neon sign over my head that only the recently deceased members of the animal kingdom can see. Now I'm supposed to play camp counselor with every dead critter that limps into my room?

Even in death, animals find me irresistible.

Being popular is a burden.

15

Another Wednesday has dawned.

Which means, in addition to my many other troubles, I will go hungry today.

Because nothing, and I mean nothing, can compel me to put Beefarooni into my body.

Beefarooni is the mixed-breed mutt of school lunches. It is a travesty of colossal proportions wrapped in a veil of tomato sauce and guile.

Plus, I'm unclear on the rules of what dead animals are going to show up next. But until I am, I'm on a strict diet of items that were not formerly alive. Mostly Doritos and Mountain Dew. The last thing I need is some Beefarooni cow showing up and getting its ghost-gunk on my bed sheets.

Apparently, my dead chicken and dead rhino compatriots do not care about such matters. Because they are scarfing the Beefarooni from my lunch tray with verve.

"Please quit touching stuff," I hiss at them. "You're going to attract unwanted attention."

But they don't. It is possible I'm the only one that can see them scarfing my lunch in plain sight. Even Darvish does not seem to notice.

Darvish shakes his brown paper bag at me and smiles. "Why don't you just bring your lunch from home on Wednesdays?" he asks me.

"Because that's what they want," I reply. "I'm not a stooge of the system."

He is eating crackers with some type of beige goo. Hummus, I believe. I'm not sure. I am not versed in the goo-shaped food products our generation so relishes.

"If you say so," he says. "Any new ideas about the dead rhino mystery?"

"That's a fair question," says Tater Tot between mouthfuls. "You making any progress on my case or what?"

I ignore the rhino and roll my eyes at Darvish. "Me?" I scold. "As my loyal sidekick, it is your job to brainstorm solutions while I am otherwise engaged."

"I'm not your sidekick," he says.

My sidekick gets mouthy sometimes. It is adorable.

He looks at my half-eaten entrée. "I thought you hated Beefarooni."

I am about to explain how Beefarooni is a black mark on the nutritional standards of our nation. How this blight on our health and taste buds may well be grounds for legal action against the Department of Education. And how my ghostly companions do not seem to care.

But before I can explain the mystery of the vanishing Beefarooni, I am interrupted. By Edwin Willoughby.

As you probably already know, Edwin Willoughby is the kid in my class who can touch his elbow with his tongue. He is pretty much world famous for this skill. That and his pit bull named Alfred make him A-OK in my book.

"Hey, Darvish," he says. "Can I borrow your math notes?"

Darvish shrugs and eats another cracker. "I no longer take notes."

"Um . . . what?" says Edwin Willoughby.

"Instead of taking notes," explains Darvish, "I use this." He extracts something long and thin from his shirt pocket.

"That's a pen," says Edwin Willoughby.

"No, it's not," says Darvish.

"Oh man, give me a break." Edwin sighs and looks to the heavens. Which is distressing, because he has clearly eaten the Beefarooni. The early symptoms of gastric distress are making themselves known.

"It's not a pen?" asks Edwin. I admire his persistence in the face of Beefarooni-induced anguish.

"No," insists Darvish. "It is a *spy* pen. With built-in ultrasonic recording capability."

"Oh," says Edwin Willoughby.

"I now record Ms. Yardley's lessons for future playback. Instead of taking notes."

"Why do you do that?" asks Edwin Willoughby.

Darvish pulls a banana from his lunch sack. He begins peeling it. "Because there is a student who sits near me who talks too much. A student who gets me in trouble with constant chattering. A student who makes it impossible for me to take notes."

I nod my head in understanding. It is kind of him not to name names in mixed company. But it doesn't take a rocket scientist to know he's talking about Sami Mulpepper. That girl is quite the chatterbox.

Edwin rubs his face with his palm in frustration. Uh-oh. The Beefarooni sweats have begun.

"Okay, then," he says, gritting his teeth. "Can I borrow your spy pen? With built-in ultrasonic recording capability?"

Darvish reluctantly surrenders the device to Edwin

Willoughby. "Fine," he says. "Just give it back by the end of the day."

Edwin Willoughby snatches the contraption and walks away. Darvish looks at me.

"Did you figure out which student I was talking about?" he asks.

I give him a knowing smile. "I'm way ahead of you, buddy."

He chews his banana. His eyes fall to my lunch tray.

"Hey, good for you," he says. "You finished your lunch."

I look to my now-empty tray. "I didn't eat it."

"Okay," says Darvish.

It's pointless to argue. I look to my right, where Drumstick and Tater Tot sit.

"That's some of the best rhino chow I've had in ages!" Tater Tot licks her mouth.

"Me too!" squawks the chicken. He rubs his stomach with his flattened flipperlike wings.

They clearly don't know what they're saying. It's obvious Beefarooni delirium has started to set in.

Even the dead are not immune.

16

I feel quite certain that, if I could find a moment's peace, I could figure out Tater Tot's ghostly afterlife dilemma lickety-split. But there are a multitude of interruptions continually vying for my attention:

1. My teacher's ongoing attempts to educate me. She never seems to tire of it.
2. An oral research report that looms over me like a specter.
3. Constantly fending off hugs from an overly affectionate dead chicken.
4. Cleaning up soot stains left behind by a crispy rhinoceros.
5. Spoon-feeding suggestions for improved side-kicking techniques to Darvish.

The demands on my time are endless. I can't concentrate. I can't get a moment to myself. I fear there is no lickety-split to be found. Which means no solution for my newly deceased animal companions. Which would be a bummer. For them and for me.

Luckily for me, I have a secret hideout that nobody can infiltrate.

It is called the shower.

Nobody dares disturb me here. Because they recognize the sanctity of this space. Because they acknowledge the privacy and respect that is due this watery fortress of solitude.

Also, because I am naked.

This Grim Reaper character has done a number on me. He has cursed me into being a conduit for recently deceased animals with unfinished business. It seems these spirits know right where to find me. I wonder if there are others with this ability. And if so, do they also use the shower as a retreat from the undead? And if so, what kind of madness is this wreaking on their water bill?

So many unanswered questions.

I try to clear my head as the steam rises around me. According to Darvish's theory, Tater Tot has come to me for a reason. She claims that the fire was set on purpose. She postulates that she heard somebody in the rhino enclosure right before the fire began. Somebody with foul intent. Apparently, if I simply solve the rhino's murder, her unfinished business in the mortal world will be resolved and she will move on to a better place. Like heaven. Or Valhalla. Or Cleveland. Anywhere but here.

It is time to get organized. It is time to put my agile brain to the task.

Perhaps if I list all the clues, the solution will make itself known.

Clue #1: A rhino is dead.

Clue #2: I have no clues beyond this.

It is possible there are forces at work that are stopping my agile brain from functioning at its best. I blame the Beefarooni. Even though I didn't eat it, perhaps just being around it has had a vicarious dumbing-down effect on me. From now on, I shall call this effect Beefarooni Brain. It is unclear if Beefarooni Brain is a real thing or a figment of my overworked imagination.

What is clear is that I am no closer to a solution than when I started this shower. My fingers have pruned up and I have nothing to show for it. It is possible that this rhino will never get to Cleveland now.

In the middle of these depressing thoughts, I feel it. A cold tingle that starts at the base of my spine and moves up from there. In spite of the warm water, the hairs on my arms stand on end. I feel unknown eyes watching me. I am not alone.

I turn and see it. A sinister shadow looms against my shower curtain. A hairy black hand reaches out and yanks the curtain aside.

"AAAAAAHHHHHHHHHH!" I scream and shield my eyes from what I feel is certain doom.

"You've been in there for weeks!" says a deep voice. "Are you planning to emerge sometime this century? I need a little help out here, if you don't mind."

I open my eyes. And I see it.

It is not certain doom. It is a gorilla. It looks like this:

As you can see, it is completely soaked from head to toe.

It has a large shark clamped on to its butt.

Green mist swirls at its feet.

It is looking expectantly at me.

And while live gorillas with live sharks chewing on their butts and green mist swirling at their feet may be commonplace in more savvy and cultured parts of the country like Cleveland, in the bathrooms of Middling Falls, they are rare.

Which can mean only one thing. This gorilla is dead. And so is the shark.

It also means one other thing. They have no regard for the sanctity of this space. For the privacy and respect that is due this watery fortress of solitude. Or for the fact that I am naked.

17

We are at the zoo.

Eating snow cones.

"This is yummy!" says Drumstick, scarfing his blue raspberry snow cone enthusiastically.

The rhino nods. "It is quite the tasty treat."

"You think *this* tastes good?" snorts the gorilla. "I once climbed for three solid months to eat snow from the frost-shrouded peaks of Mount Karisimbi. It tasted like world peace drizzled with honey and sprinkles. This is nothing!"

The snow-cone guy looked at me funny when I ordered four snow cones, but if I cared what people thought of me, I wouldn't be where I am today.

Which is at the zoo. Dad dropped me off. He seemed pleased that I had taken an interest in learning about animals. If he only knew. Plus, the gorilla left a puddle of water on the bathroom floor and I got the blame for it. So I think my dad was happy to have me out of the house.

The gorilla. He tried to explain his predicament to me. The shark did, too, but it was hard to understand him with a mouthful of gorilla butt. So their story was a bit confusing. That's when I called Darvish, because he speaks Confusing quite fluently. But he didn't answer his phone. Which is rude, if you ask me. When a dead gorilla interrupts your best friend's shower, you pick up the phone.

I decided I needed visual inspiration. And what better inspiration than where it all happened?

Which is at the zoo.

I suspect that the antidote to my Beefarooni Brain™ is kiwi-lime snow cone. Because I am clearheaded at last. Clearheaded enough to remember that I am a man of big, bold moves. Clearheaded enough to realize that staking out the scene of the crime is my next big, bold move.

"Let's take a closer look at that Gorilla House," I say.

Only, there is a problem at the scene of the crime. Part of the zoo has been roped off. The rhinoceros exhibit is closed. And the Gorilla House is closed. And the Oceanarium is closed. The universe is conspiring against my big, bold moves.

But I'm here on semiofficial business. So I ignore the ropes.

"Hey, kid! You can't be back here!"

It is a big, bold security guard. He is big in girth rather than height, likely owing to a steady diet of corn dogs and funnel cakes. He is bold because he is standing in the way of my semiofficial authority.

"Back behind the rope, kid," he says, pointing.

"What's going on?" I ask.

"None of your beeswax," he says. "That's what."

"This is discrimination," I say. "I'm being oppressed under the thumb of The Man."

"What man?" he asks.

"You!" I explain. "Where were you on the night in question?"

He rubs the temples of his balloon-shaped head. "Probably here, not making enough money for this nonsense."

I make a mental note on this suspicious charac-ter: *Guard too pudgy to commit murder.* But I stand my ground. "My taxes pay for this zoo," I say. "You work for me, good sir. As such, I will thank you kindly to heed my authority in this matter."

He does not heed my authority in this matter. Instead, he escorts me by the arm and returns me to the safety of the snow-cone stand. "I'm pretty sure little kids don't pay taxes," he says. "Plus, taxes don't pay for the zoo. Admission prices do." He waddles back to his ropes with a huff.

Curses. This is all Darvish's fault. If he were here, he could probably jury-rig some sort of explosion to distract the guard. It's dangerous work, but I'd be willing to sacrifice him to the cause. I could then slip by unnoticed on nimble cat paws. Instead, I've been fast-talked and manhandled by the short rotund arm of the law. Which means we can't get anywhere near the actual scene of the crime.

And the zoo closes in an hour. Which means we are running out of time.

Plus, Tater Tot wants another snow cone. "I'm getting a headache," I mutter, rubbing my eyes.

"Quit being a baby," says the gorilla, thumping his chest for emphasis. "I once got hit in the head with forty-seven coconuts! Not regular coconuts, mind you, coconuts from a rare breed of acid-coconut tree! I barely felt a thing!"

The shark rolls his eyes.

This gorilla has proved to be just as obnoxious as the rhino in his own special way.

I take a deep breath. "Okay," I say. "Tell me again how you got out of the Gorilla House. And how you wound up with a shark nibbling your bottom."

"It wasn't my fault," the gorilla says, furrowing his thick brow. "Somebody opened my cage."

"I'm telling you, there are sinister workings afoot," chimes in Tater Tot. "Somebody's out to get us."

"You said somebody set that fire," I confirm.

"Uh, yeah!" she says, tapping her foot. "Somebody sinister! That fire killed me completely dead!"

I turn to the gorilla. "And you were killed by a shark?"

He turns around to reveal the shark chewing noisily on his hindquarters. "This? This is nothing! I once had a panther chew off my whole leg! I beat the panther to a pulp, crawled inside his stomach, retrieved my leg, and sewed it back on with nothing but vines!"

"Thwapptleverrlappenlled!" the shark mumbles.

"It did too happen!" the gorilla tells the shark. "It happened on several different occasions!"

I shake my head. "So how did you die?"

"I drowned," he says. "Not my fault I can't swim."

"But how . . ."

"Not my fault! Somebody opened my cage!"

"We've established that."

"Look here, you little—" he starts.

Tater Tot steps up to the gorilla, towering over him

like a small pointy-nosed mountain. "Sheesh! Dial it down a notch! Rexxie is just trying to get the facts straight. There's no cause to get huffy."

"Yeah," squawks Drumstick. "Don't be huffy to Rexxie."

"Yeah," I murmur. "Rexxie."

The gorilla backs off. "Okay. Sorry. Dying takes a lot out of you." He blows out his cheeks and presses his knuckles to the ground. "I'll start at the beginning. I've never been outside my enclosure, right? Not since I was first brought to this place from the wild. So when somebody opened up the door, I went out. I'm curious by nature, okay? And when I came to the Oceanarium display, I went inside."

"And you fell into the shark tank?" I ask.

"Thwightlinthwothwiythwankthwankthwouth-erythwuch!" gurgles the shark.

"The water looked refreshing," says the gorilla. "What can I say? I'm a sucker for refreshing-looking water."

"And the shark attacked you and tried to kill you?"

"He wishes!" snorts the gorilla. "One time I got stampeded by a herd of wildebeests while the wilde-beests were being stampeded by a herd of elephants while the elephants were being chased by a pack of wild dogs! Nobody survived except me!"

"That seems made-up," I say.

"Another time, I fell a thousand feet off a cliff

while wrestling a crocodile and used the crocodile's mouth as a parachute to land safely at the bottom. This shark is nothing." He points at the shark. "See all that bruising around the snout? That's all me. I gave him a good pummeling, I did!"

"Thwimmeethwabwake," says the shark around a snoutful of ape heinie.

"Fine," I say. "And while you were pummeling the shark to death, you drowned."

The gorilla nods. "Yeah. But it's not my fault, is it? Somebody opened my cage."

This ape is holding out. Time to ask the hard questions. I look him sternly in the eye. "Do you or the shark owe anybody money?"

He looks confused.

"My best friend asked you a question," chimes in Drumstick. His beak has turned raspberry blue.

The gorilla shrugs. "What's money?"

I keep the pressure on. "Does anybody owe you money?"

Once again, he claims to have no working knowledge of basic currency.

I throw my hands up in exasperation. "Can either of you think of anybody who would want you out of the way?" I ask.

"Obviously somebody who hates animals," says Tater Tot. "What other possible reason could there be to make all this disappear?" She holds her rhino-arms out and twirls in a circle. "Look at me. I'm a rare beauty."

"You think you're rare?" pipes up the gorilla. "I'm so rare, I'm practically extinct! There's less than one of me left in existence! I know saber-toothed tigers that are more common than I am!"

I sit down in defeat and finish my snow cone. It tastes like kiwi-lime and failure. I'm astute enough to realize that my clue-hunting trip to the zoo is a bust.

How could Darvish not answer his phone? Because I really need an explosives expert right about now.

And a best friend.

18

Friday morning dawns, and the school halls are filled with excited chatter about the upcoming Evening of Enchantment Dance. Who's wearing what. Who's going with whom. It is a tedious business.

Judging by their vapid jabber, my classmates have no awareness of the bigger issue at hand: that I have still made no headway ridding myself of the deluge of dead animals following me around.

With so many supernatural forces conspiring against me, it is a small miracle that I am not more discouraged. But as I sign up for my research report slot, I am not frowning the frown of the discouraged. Instead, I am smiling the smile of the clever and self-assured.

Because I have come up with a brilliant strategy for tackling my research report.

It is called the Take-the-Last-Presentation-Slot Strategy. Which is a snazzy name for a strategy, if I do say so myself.

By picking the last possible presentation slot on the sheet, I have given myself until next Friday to present my report. A full week. This gives me more time than anybody else.

Some people would call this procrastination. Other people would call this laziness. I call this basic common sense. Does that make me a genius among mere mortals? A higher life-form? A king among men? Who am I to say? History will judge.

I just wish my mom and dad could see all this common sense in action. They would beg me to own a chocolate Lab.

Sami Mulpepper has signed up for the first presentation slot. Which means she has to present first thing next week. It is one more example of how book smarts cannot compete with street smarts in the real world.

Of course, my leisure time is much more in demand than hers. She doesn't have three dead animals hounding her. Four, if you count the shark. I'm not sure I do. He is not a sparkling conversationalist and mostly just continues to gnaw on the gorilla's butt.

As we enter the classroom, Ms. Yardley reminds

us that there's still time to sign up for the Evening of Enchantment decorating committee. No thank you. I have had enough glitter to last two lifetimes.

"Where were you last night?" I ask Darvish as we take our seats. "I called you."

"At home," he says. "My phone died."

"Well, thanks to you, I had a dreadful night." I fill him in on the interruption of my shower, the appearance of the gorilla, and our explosionless exploits at the zoo.

"Oh my gosh . . . a gorilla?" he says, reaching into his backpack. "Did you see this morning's newspaper?"

"Of course not," I respond. "It is always filled with death and destruction. Which depresses me. Plus, the news is almost never about me."

"This story is," he says, passing the paper to me. "Kind of."

I grab the newspaper. The headline reads: EVENING TRAGEDY AT MIDDLING ZOO.

I yawn. They don't need to tell me about tragedy. I barely got any beauty sleep because Drumstick, Tater Tot, the gorilla, and the shark are taking up so much room in my bed, there is barely any space left for me. Not only am I the only one who can see or hear them, I seem to be the only one who is affected by the sheer square footage they take up. If that's not a tragedy, I don't know what is.

At least I have something to share for current events. I take the newspaper and saunter to the front.

Ms. Yardley looks skeptical. "Rex? You have a current event to read?"

"You betcha," I answer. "Prepare to dispense some extra credit."

"Is it appropriate?" she asks. "It's not appropriate, is it?" She hesitates, looking unsure. I take advantage of her slow reflexes and clear my throat. Raising my rich tenor tones to the rafters, I read the article aloud to the class.

EVENING TRAGEDY AT MIDDLING ZOO

It was discovered early last evening that an adult mountain gorilla had escaped from its enclosure at the Middling Zoo. The remains of the gorilla were found shortly after in the shark tank of the zoo's Oceanarium enclosure, along with a dead bull shark.

"We do not suspect foul play," said zoo consultant Haughtry Vain. "It is likely that the gorilla's enclosure lock failed. Upon exploring the grounds, it wandered into the shark tank, where an epic shark-gorilla battle ensued."

The gorilla's cause of death is undetermined, but drowning is suspected. The shark's cause of death appears to be a result of the gorilla encounter.

"This is the problem with these old-fashioned cages," said Vain. *"Locks fail. Bars rust. My organization is working with the zoo to create newer, safer enclosures."*

Ms. Vain's organization is Cageless Enclosure Solutions, which works with animal parks and sanctuaries to create wide-open, cage-free animal enclosures. The Middling Zoo has not yet decided to move forward with the project, but if they do, Ms. Vain and her company will undertake a massive renovation of all zoo enclosures.

Perhaps the recent tragic events will spur the zoo to action. But not everyone agrees with this solution.

"This type of thing is to be expected when you cage animals," said Talon Smithfield, president of a local organization called PUPAE, or People United to Protect Animals Everywhere. *"The answer isn't better cages. The answer is that these rare and majestic beasts should be returned to the wild where they belong."*

In the meantime, measures are being taken to ensure the safety of the animals and the public.

"All enclosure locks are being examined for defects," said Vain. *"We do not expect any future problems."*

This marks the second recent tragedy at the zoo, following this week's fire that killed a Sumatran rhinoceros.

"Very good," says Ms. Yardley, looking pleasantly surprised. "Very appropriate."

But *was* it very good?

Was it appropriate?

Because I look up from the article. And I see Holly Creskin.

Giggling.

19

"I brought that article in for current events," says Darvish, opening his lunch sack. "Me!"

As often happens, Darvish is fixating on the wrong thing.

"Then that worked out perfectly," I say.

"For myself to read! That was my extra credit you stole."

My poor chum. He should know as well as anybody—you cannot steal extra credit. Extra credit is in the public domain. It's like air, clean tap water, and the pursuit of happiness. It belongs to everybody. It floats in the breeze, available for public consumption by anyone with the chutzpah to take advantage of it.

"Pay attention, man!" I remind him. "Someone is murdering animals!"

"But the article said that no foul play is suspected."

"Don't be a rube your whole life, Darvish! That's subterfuge! Trickery! Propaganda!" I take a bite of my grilled cheese sandwich for emphasis. "Someone is opening cages. Someone is setting fires. Tater Tot and Sea-Monkey said so themselves!"

"Sea-Monkey?"

"It just came to me," I say.

"Because he fell into the Oceanarium tank. And has a shark on his butt. That's funny."

"Thank you."

"Where are they, anyway?" he asks. "Are they here?"

"No, we had a late and fruitless night, thanks to you. They stayed home to rest."

"How can ghosts get tired?" he asks.

"Focus!" I sputter impatiently. "Somebody is deliberately picking them off. And who would want to kill a gorilla and a rhino? The guard is too pudgy!"

Darvish shrugs. I slap my hand over my face. This kid is of no use to me. I'm seriously considering promoting Drumstick to role of sidekick and best friend.

I turn back to Darvish. "A notorious hater of animals, that's who! Namely . . . Holly Creskin!"

"What?" he cries. "That's crazy. A kid is not break-ing into the zoo and killing animals."

I have lost all patience with Darvish. "Do you know any torture techniques? Thumbscrews, stretch-ing on the rack, those types of skills?"

"No," he says.

"You will have to learn. We may need them. Come on." I stand up and head across the cafeteria. The time has come for more chutzpah.

"Where are we going?" he calls, chasing after me.

"To interrogate Holly Creskin."

20

We sit down across from the culprit.

At this close range, I can see the malevolence burning within her. The animal-hating, rhino-burning, gorilla-drowning malevolence.

"Hi, Darvish! Hi, Rex!" she says, surprised at our presence. That's the thing about the guilty. They always look surprised. "Hey, are you guys going to the Evening of Enchantment dance next week?"

I scoff at the thought. "Do not be ludicrous."

"That's too bad," she chirps. "It's going to be so fun!"

I have no time for social niceties. "Your attempts to divert my attention are pointless, Holly Creskin. We do not want to talk about dances."

"Oh," she says. "Okay. What do you want?"

"Your confession," I say. "Why did you do it?"

"Do what?"

"Don't play coy with me, sister. I've known you were a hater of animals for a long time, but I never thought you would stoop this low."

"What are you talking about?" she asks, pushing her tray to the side. "I love animals."

"Don't give me that. I am the only one at this table who has a well-documented love of animals. I've wanted a dog for forever."

"It's practically all he ever talks about," Darvish supplies helpfully.

"Exactly!" I nod. "Yet every time I bring it up with you, you wrinkle your nose in a distasteful fashion. And do you know why?"

"Yes," she says.

I level an accusing finger at her. "Because you hate animals!"

"No," says Holly Creskin. "It's because I don't like dogs."

"What?"

"Cats rule. Dogs drool. And dogs are the only animals you ever talk about."

"It's true, Rex," says Darvish. "You're kind of obsessed. Chocolate Lab this. Chocolate Lab that."

"Don't you dare take the name of that majestic creature in vain." I turn back to Holly Creskin. "So, you haven't brought about the demise of any zoo animals recently?"

"What?" she cries. "No! I love animals! I love unicorns and pegasuses and rainbows and unicorns—"

I interrupt her. "Rainbows are not animals."

"And all that other stuff is not real," chimes in Darvish.

"I love real animals too! I love kitties and ponies and kitties—"

"How do you feel about gorillas?" I ask. "Or rhinos?"

"I love all animals except dogs!" she claims.

Dang, she's good.

"I'm even a member of People United to Protect Animals Everywhere." She lifts up her purse, which has a large PUPAE button proudly displayed.

I stand up on the lunch table to make myself appear bigger. I am a Saint Bernard in a cafeteria full of teacup poodles. I can tell the technique is working because Holly Creskin looks terrified of me. As she should.

"If this cockamamie story is true," I shout, "and that's a big IF, then why did you giggle at the end of my current event today?"

"MY current event," interjects Darvish. That kid cannot let something go.

"Let's stay on topic," I tell him. I turn back to Holly Creskin. "It wasn't exactly a funny article. More horribly tragic than funny. Why the giggle?"

Holly Creskin rolls her eyes and looks embarrassed. "Oh, that!"

I am prepared to use Holly Creskin's spork as a thumbscrew. But I sense a confession forthcoming. Perhaps torture will not be needed after all.

"Because I *know* Talon Smithfield," she says. "The guy you mentioned in the article. He's the president of People United to Protect Animals Everywhere. He's very tall. And so passionate about the rights of animals! He's in high school."

"Isn't that the guy who hangs out near PetPlanet begging for money?" I ask Darvish.

"PUPAE," he says. "Oh yeah, maybe."

"He wanted to charge us fifty-nine ninety-nine to join his group?"

"I don't remember. I was distracted by the firehouse tacos. And you getting cursed."

I turn back to Holly Creskin. "You gave him fifty-nine ninety-nine to join that group?" I ask. "What would possess you?"

She laughs. "No, silly. My parents paid for it. They like animals, too. In fact, my dad is the presi—"

I cut her off. "So what if you know Talon Smithfield? Why would that make you giggle?" I am confused. It's a sensation I'm experiencing a lot lately.

She giggles again.

"Because she *likes* him," says Darvish.

At this, Holly Creskin dissolves afresh into peals of laughter that will not stop. She is now useless to me as a suspect.

I step off the table and walk away, leaving her to her giggle-fit.

Unknowingly, she has cleared herself of all suspicion.

Because murderers don't giggle. They laugh maniacally. Everybody knows this.

21

I am at an emotional, spiritual, and metaphysical standstill.

I am no closer to figuring out why a rhino and a gorilla (and a shark) have had their lives in captivity cut tragically short.

I am no closer to ridding myself of these respective soot-covered, flea-bitten (and barnacle-encrusted) houseguests from the great beyond.

Since it is the weekend, I decide to do something about it. The one thing that will distract them from their predicament. The one thing that will distract me from the crushing stalemate in which I currently find myself.

Pizza party.

"Your best private room, my good man," I say.

We are standing at the shoe desk of the BowlTastic. It is Middling Falls' premier bowling and pizza destination. The guy behind the counter looks at me like I've lost my mind. It is a look that I have grown accustomed to over the years.

"A private room for one person?" the shoe man asks.

"Possibly," I say evasively. I am veiled in a shroud of mystery and I prefer to keep it that way.

He takes a deep breath. "Whatever, kid. The birthday party room is empty today. You can sit in there. Order your food at the bar."

As private accommodations go, these are a bit juvenile. And sad. There is a faded jungle mural on the wall. Papier-mâché toucans hang from the ceiling tiles. But it is private, so we are free to talk without me looking like a deranged loon.

Ridiculously, the BowlTastic does not stock rhino or gorilla food. So, I make the best selections I can with my compatriots in mind. I place the pizza before them. "Anchovies and spinach," I say proudly. "They were fresh out of bananas, chicken food, and whatever rhinos eat."

"Nah," says Tater Tot. "I'm not hungry."

"Me neither," says Sea-Monkey, sighing. "I can go

days without food. One time, I spent six months eating nothing but fire ants. Do you know how small a fire ant is? They're tiny."

The shark just continues to gnaw Sea-Monkey's hindquarters.

Only Drumstick seems enthusiastic with my choice. "Thanks, buddy! Ooh, look! You got my favorite! Triangles!"

If I'd known that nobody else was going to eat, I'd have just gotten cheese. My consideration and self-sacrifice is wasted on this group.

I sit next to my small mountain of picked-off toppings. And chew my triangle. Drumstick pecks noisily at my side.

But the others have a faraway look. They gaze longingly at the poorly painted jungle mural.

Perhaps they are not spurning my consideration and self-sacrifice on purpose.

Perhaps they are just as sad to be here as I am vexed to have them here.

Perhaps they are not here by choice.

Perhaps an afterlife paradise of grassy plains and lush treetops (and undersea reefs) respectively awaits each of them.

Perhaps I am not the only one that has been cursed.

Darvish suspects that if we can solve the mystery surrounding their unnatural deaths, then their spirits will move on. If he is right, then they are stuck here. Doomed to the purgatory of Middling Falls. Until the unfinished business that tethers them here is complete.

So I've got to figure this out once and for all. Who would want to murder these guys?

I reach out and scratch Tater Tot behind her charred ear.

I rub Sea-Monkey's eternally drenched fur.

I attach the pizza box to the end of a long broom and gently stroke the shark from a safe distance.

I put my arm around Drumstick's two-dimensional neck.

"What are we doing, Rexxie?" asks Drumstick.

"Having a moment," I say.

"Okay, buddy."

We all stare at the jungle mural. And sigh.

22

A successful coup has transpired. My room has officially been taken over.

Darvish has commandeered my video-game console with a new game called Peanut Paradise. It involves a giant mouse setting traps for an elephant.

Apparently, it is all the rage among my age bracket. I wouldn't know. I have had no mental capacity for video games lately. My brain, once a carefree and happy-go-lucky place, is now occupied with pondering the criminal nature of man against his four-legged brethren.

Tater Tot, Sea-Monkey, and Drumstick are all waiting for their turn. Which leaves no controller for me to use. And no room for me on my own bed.

I have been ousted.

"Rexxie, will you come in here, please?" My dad is calling from the other room. His tone is stern. It suggests he is not calling me to hand out Popsicles.

"Rexxie," says Darvish. "Your dad is calling."

"Don't call me that," I say. "I'll be right back. Try to brainstorm some solutions while I'm gone."

"I'll come too," says Drumstick. "In case he's handing out Popsicles." Despite his lack of a heartbeat, Drumstick is proving to be a loyal companion. Also, he seems to love people food.

My dad is a stay-at-home dad. He is the only stay-at-home dad I know. He says that is because he is enlightened. I don't know what that means. But being enlightened seems to come with a wide array of hard work. Like cooking. And cleaning. So do not sign me up for being enlightened anytime soon.

At the moment, he is doing the laundry. And he does not look pleased.

"What is this, Rex?" he asks, holding up my soot-stained bedsheets. "Are these ashes?"

Oh boy. I don't pretend to fully understand how all this works. I'm the only one who can see the ghost animals that have come to haunt me. But it seems that their ghostly side effects are occasionally apparent to others. Like the puddles that Sea-Monkey keeps leaving everywhere. Or the soot stains from my toasty rhino compatriot.

"Ah, yes," I say, thinking on my feet. "Ashes. That may or may not be from a science project. Feel free to blame the Scientific Method."

"Oh," he says. "Well, be more careful next time."

My dad's interrogation methods are feeble. I bet good money that he doesn't even have any thumb-screws in that laundry basket. You have to feel bad for the guy.

"How ya doing, pal?" he asks me. "You seem pre-occupied lately."

I pause, internally debating my response. My dad always says I can talk to him about anything. And, I confess, I could use some advice.

I could tell him that I've been cursed by the Grim Reaper. I could tell him that ghosts are real. I could tell him that a menagerie of dead animals is using my bed-room as their layover terminal to the great unknown. I could tell him that solving the cold-blooded murder of innocent creatures rests squarely on my humble shoulders.

But these are the types of ramblings that get you locked away in the booby hatch.

So I blame the old standby. "Just school stuff." Classic.

I turn to go, but he stops me. "Speaking of school-work, how's your research report coming?"

The hairs on my arms stand on end. I feel a chill

go up my spine that has nothing to do with Drumstick rooting through the freezer nearby for Popsicles. Again, my father seems oblivious to the important things. He seems to be privy to my homework assignments but is blissfully unaware that our Popsicle supply is being pilfered right under his nose.

I clear my throat. "I'm sorry. What was that?"

"I saw the assignment sheet next to your back-pack," he says. "When I was cleaning your room."

"Ah." He is craftier than I have given him credit for. "You'll be happy to know I have taken a very mature approach to the project."

"Oh, good. I was worried you might sign up for the last presentation slot and put it off till the last second."

I chortle vaguely. The man has no faith in me.

When I return to my room, it is clear that no brain-storming has occurred while I was away. Darvish is going on three hours of Peanut Paradise.

I decide to state the obvious.

"You may have a problem with addiction," I say to him. "I hate to bring it up, but I think I need to address the elephant in the room."

"Oh sure! You betcha!" says a chipper voice. "Address me! I'm standing right here!"

I turn. There is an actual elephant. In the room. It has a big, friendly grin plastered across its face.

But there's a problem with this elephant. Other than its squeaky voice and the fact that it is in my house. This is not an elephant-shaped elephant. He has been squashed into a square shape. Like a cube. Four stubby little legs emerge from the bottom of the cube, pooled in green glowing mist.

I look over at Darvish. He is immersed in his game, unaware that a real-live dead elephant has entered the room while his eyes are glued to his fake video-game elephant.

That kid may have real problems.

23

It is clear we need a place free from distractions. A place where we can analyze the situation before us. We need to have a Meeting of the Minds.

And the old picnic table in the corner of the recess yard is perfect.

The picnic table is a death trap waiting to spring. It is a wreck of rotting wood and rusty nails. It is lousy with termites and tetanus. Hardly anyone ever goes near it. Which is exactly the kind of seclusion we require.

"Let the Meeting of the Minds commence," I say, calling us to order.

"Spirit Summit," corrects Darvish. "We agreed to call this a Spirit Summit."

"But Meeting of the Minds sounds better."

"We voted. You said Spirit Summit won."

"Darvish is right," says Tater Tot. "Play fair, now."

"That's right," agrees Sea-Monkey. "I voted for Spirit Summit. I demand my voice be heard!"

"Mweetwoo!" mumbles the shark.

"I suggested GhostCon, but nobody liked that one," chortles the elephant. "Which is finc! Spirit Summit is a nifty name, too."

I must concede to the majority vote. Only the chicken voted with me. Even the cube-shaped elephant eventually voted for Spirit Summit. I am not sure I like this new elephant.

Yesterday, after I pried Darvish away from his video game, we got the elephant's story. They say an elephant never forgets, but his recollections were murky. According to his sketchy account, he saw a shadowy figure open his enclosure. He followed a trail of peanuts into a big truck. The truck rumbled for a while, then stopped. Suddenly the walls started closing in like a trash compactor. The next thing he knew, he was dead and box-shaped.

"Sheesh," said Tater Tot, grimacing. "I thought my death was nasty."

"Yeah," I agreed, looking over the box-shaped elephant. "That's horrible."

"That?" cried Sea-Monkey. "That's nothing! I once

slipped on a banana peel, fell off a cliff, and landed headfirst in a hollowed-out tree. I was cylinder-shaped for the next month! Being cube-shaped is a dream come true compared to that!"

The elephant just laughed it off. "Aw, it's not so bad! I barely felt a thing. Maybe I blacked out in peanut-induced bliss. That sometimes happens. I love those little nuts, but boy, do they make me loopy! I'll tell you this, though. Somebody was clearly out to get me. That's when I knew I needed somebody like you to help me out! And here we all are!"

"And you didn't see who it was?" I asked.

"Golly, I'm sorry. I wish I could help more. But it was dark. And I was very focused on the peanut situation."

"I thought elephants were supposed to be smart."

"We are!" he cried. "Super smart! I can do long division in my head! Which maybe makes it short division. Not sure. And don't get me started on circus trivia! You'll never get me to shut up!"

"Then why would you just follow a random trail of peanuts?"

He blushed and looked away. "What can I say? I like peanuts. I'm a victim of my own appetite." As a result, I have named him Peanut. Trust me, it's not exactly a compliment.

And now, twenty-four hours later, we still have no

idea how our newest ghostly companion wound up in the shape he's in.

I look at the group gathered around the picnic table. "I have called us together because far-reaching and eternity-altering issues are at hand."

"I second the motion!" says the chicken.

I go on. "The kind of issues that require the utmost brainpower, maturity, and concentration."

"Where are we supposed to find someone like that?" asks Darvish. "Do you think Sami Mulpepper would help?"

"Me, Darvish. I'm talking about me."

"We're doomed."

"Objection!" says Drumstick.

"Sustained," I say. "Now, what do we know?"

"I know nothing!" says Drumstick. Everyone ignores the chicken.

"Does anyone have any new information to share?" I ask.

"This gorilla snores," says Tater Tot. "It's totally wreaking havoc on my sleep cycle."

"You think you've got problems?" says Sea-Monkey. "Try sleeping with a three-hundred-pound bull shark nibbling on your hindquarters!"

The shark just rolls his eyes.

"Does that hurt?" asks Peanut. "It looks like it hurts."

"Naw," says Sea-Monkey. "You know what hurts

when they bite? Tsetse flies, that's what. Those bites can sting for decades! This is nothing!"

"I see. I see." Peanut nods. "Why does he keep hanging on like that?"

"How's he supposed to get around?" asks the gorilla. "He doesn't have legs, does he?"

"Good point. Good point."

"I've got new information," says Darvish. Thank goodness for that. Hearing every insipid thought that comes out of their ghost mouths is not the treat for the ears that you imagine it is. I was about to clonk some ghost heads together.

"Check this out." Darvish flops this morning's *Middling Falls Daily Spew* onto the table. On the front page is the headline ZOO'S MISSING INDIAN ELEPHANT FOUND AT CAR CRUSHING YARD.

"Car crusher?" I ask.

Darvish shudders. "Those giant car-squashing machines that they use at the junkyard. They turn old cars into little metal cubes."

Yikes. So that's how it happened. Whoever is behind this has a heart as black as a panther's heinie. And for all I know, the panther's heinie is the next one on the chopping block. I clench my fist and resolve to not let that happen to the panther's heinie. Or any other creature's heinie.

"Maybe we can get into the rhino cage or the elephant enclosure," suggests Darvish. "To look for footprints or clues or something."

I shake my head. "I told you, getting near the scene of the crime is impossible. They have the empty enclosures roped off. They are guarded by a surprisingly efficient hobbit. Honestly, Darvish, if you're going to be my sidekick, you're going to have to listen more closely."

"I'm not your sidekick."

"Please stay on topic," I remind him. "This is a Spirit Summit."

"There has to be something that connects these animals together," says Darvish.

So we brainstorm. Our brains collide in a hurricane of ideas. Our imaginations swirl in a vortex of possibilities. It is a true Meeting of the Minds. Or Spirit Summit. Or GhostCon. Or whatever.

Here are the things we come up with during our brainstorming session that Tater Tot, Sea-Monkey, and Peanut all have in common:

They all lived at the zoo.

A mysterious somebody opened all of their cages or enclosures before they met their untimely fate.

They are all mammals.

The shark is not a mammal. He insisted this be

included in the list. But since his death seems to be a by-product of the gorilla's murder and therefore unintentional, I rule it as irrelevant.

The elephant likes peanuts.

Beyond that, there seems to be no clear connection between them. Perhaps we need some better brains. None of these similarities seems important or grounds for death.

"What else do we know?" I ask.

"I know nothing!" says Drumstick. Everyone ignores the chicken.

"Well, I can tell you the TV crews are all over this," says Darvish. "The news lady was interviewing the president of the zoo board last night."

"And?"

"It's in here." He thumbs through the newspaper. "Here it is. *'Timothy Creskin, the president of the zoo board, blames rusty locks for the tragic events. "This is a serious situation," he stated firmly. "I plan to take legal action against the company that manufactures the gates. These animals escaped on their own and their deaths were a series of tragic but isolated accidents."'*

"Accident, schmaccident," says Tater Tot.

"He refuses to close the zoo," says Darvish. "He assures the public that no foul play was involved."

"But we know differently," I say.

"But we don't have any proof," Darvish cries. "We need evidence."

"Okay. What else do a rhino, a gorilla, and an elephant have in common?" I ask. "What else do we know?"

"I know nothing!" says Drumstick. Everyone ignores the chicken.

But Drumstick has cut to the heart of the situation.

We know nothing.

I bang my head against the picnic table, risking a nasty bout of tetanus in the process.

I must admit, living dangerously suits me. It's frustrating at times. And splintery. But despite the hopelessness of our situation and wood chips sticking out of my forehead, I feel somehow more alive than ever before.

24

In my years of wandering this earth, I have learned many things.

For example, sometimes the storm is followed by the calm.

Sometimes it is darkest before the dawn.

And sometimes, when things seem at their darkest, more darkness can come and eclipse that already dark darkness, making it darker than the blackest midnight and obscuring all hope from sight. Forever.

Such a day is today. Because today, the research reports start.

Sami Mulpepper takes her place at the front of the classroom. A smile washes over her face. She is in her glory.

"Endangered Species," she proclaims. "By Samantha Mulpepper."

I will confess to you that her research is thorough. Her eyes sparkle with passion as she embraces her topic. Her presentation quality contains that special something. However, I do my level best to tune her out. I have bigger fish to fry. Huge fish. Like grouper. Or sea bass.

While Sami Mulpepper lectures us on the troubles of habitat encroachment facing Sumatran rhinos and California condors, I think about Tater Tot.

While she sermonizes on the dangers of poaching that threaten Amur tigers and mountain gorillas, I ruminate on Sea-Monkey and the shark-shaped growth attached to his hindquarters.

While she pontificates on the perils facing snow leopards, hawksbill turtles, Indian elephants, and spoon-billed sandpipers, I stew on Peanut.

And then it hits me like a two-ton, cube-shaped pachyderm.

I turn to Darvish. "Not just rhino," I say. "SUMATRAN rhino."

"Huh?"

"Not just gorilla," I say, my certainty growing. "MOUNTAIN gorilla."

"What are you talking about?"

"Not just elephant," I proclaim. "INDIAN elephant!"

I stand on my desk to make myself appear larger and more impressive.

"ENDANGERED SPECIES!" I bellow. "LET IT GO OUT ACROSS THE LAND! I HAVE DONE IT! ALL YE WHO BEAR WITNESS, BE IMPRESSED AND TREMBLE!"

The room has gone silent. This can happen when

a large and impressive breed like myself makes his presence known.

I have seen the light.

I have connected the dots.

I have put two and two together. And the answer is not four.

The answer is *Endangered Species*.

"YOU TAKE YOUR SEAT RIGHT NOW, REX DEXTER!"

It is Sami Mulpepper. She has climbed to the top of Ms. Yardley's desk. Her presence looms over me like some sort of auburn-haired Siberian husky. She is a Great Dane to my Chihuahua. I tuck tail in the presence of this superior predator and quickly take my seat.

Ms. Yardley is stunned. But only for a moment. A wide smile crosses her face. She is clearly pleased by my recent flash of inspiration. "Sami," she says. "Twenty extra-credit points. Please continue your wonderful report."

Sami Mulpepper eyes me. Then she continues her well-researched oration from atop the towering roost of Ms. Yardley's desk.

I am cowed in the face of Sami Mulpepper's authority.

Also, I think I am in love.

25

I do not have time to entertain thoughts of love. I do not have the wherewithal to contemplate amour. I do not have the time to mull over the chestnut hair and can-do attitude of Sami Mulpepper.

I have had a complete and utter brain wave. A brain typhoon. A brain tsunami. I must bring my sidekick up to speed.

"I figured it out," I tell Darvish.

"Figured out what?" he asks through bites of his peanut butter and banana sandwich. "How to make a fool of yourself in the middle of oral presentations?"

"I have not made a fool of myself," I assure him. "I have made a major breakthrough."

"Ignore him," says Drumstick. "Tell me."

"Yeah! Spill," says Tater Tot. "We're all ears."

My lunch table is crowded. Word about the alleged "deliciousness" of my school lunch has gotten out among my dead amigos. Because Drumstick, Tater Tot, Sea-Monkey, and Peanut have all joined me for lunch in the hopes of mooching more Beefarooni. As it is not Wednesday, they have been disappointed by the cafeteria's lack of Beefarooni. This has not stopped them from helping themselves to my Nacho Surprise.

"I've figured out what Tater Tot, Sea-Monkey, and Peanut all have in common," I tell Darvish. "They're all endangered."

"Of course!" Darvish says.

I grin the grin of victory. "Somebody is wiping out endangered species."

"Told you I was rare," says Tater Tot.

"Not as rare as me!" says Sea-Monkey. "I'm practically nonexistent!"

"Oh wow. Oh wow," says Peanut. "Nice job! Hey, pass the salsa, would you?"

"The newspaper said they were rare!" says Darvish. "I just never made the connection!"

I nod at Darvish from across the table. "It's not your fault. We cannot all have the nimble mind and uncanny brainpower of an undiscovered genius."

"Yeah," says Darvish. "Good thing Sami Mulpepper is in our class."

I sigh. "I would have reached this inevitable conclusion of my own accord. However, I will confess that her oral report may have inadvertently pointed me in the right direction."

Darvish laughs. "That's generous. You should tell her that."

"I do not want to give her a big head. Let's be honest, nobody needs that burden. But should the opportunity arise, I may convey how much I enjoyed her report."

"Well, get ready to convey," says Tater Tot. "Because here she comes now."

It's true. Sami Mulpepper is waltzing over to our table. Bold as brass, she sits right down next to me. Plopping herself right on my chicken.

Or in my chicken.

Or through my chicken.

I'm not sure of the grammar of ghost-chicken sitting.

"Hi, Darvish," she says. "Hello, Rex."

"Hey, Sami," says Darvish.

"Um . . ." I say.

"Did you like my report today?" she asks.

"It was amazing," says Darvish. "Rex was just saying what a revelation it was. Weren't you, Rex?"

"Um . . ." I say.

"Brrrr." Sami shivers. "It's cold over here."

"Sure is," says Darvish gleefully. He is enjoying this moment far too much. "Isn't it, Rex?"

"Um . . ." I say.

Of course Sami Mulpepper is cold. She is chilly because her seat is occupied by a ghost chicken. The temperature drop is because she is seated in dead farmyard poultry. Her sudden chill is a by-product of her close encounter with the otherworldly.

But she doesn't know any of this. Nor should she. I am about to clear my throat and suggest that she find a seat in a warmer and less chicken-occupied part of the cafeteria. But my voice leaves me. Because that's when she says something that nobody, and I mean nobody, could have predicted.

"Rex, would you like to go to the Evening of Enchantment dance with me?"

"Um . . ." I say.

"Um . . ." I say again.

"Um . . ." I say a third time. I am nothing if not thorough.

"I believe the word you're looking for is yes," prompts Sami Mulpepper.

I clear my throat. "Okay."

"Perfect," she says with a smile. "My mom and I will pick you up at seven o'clock sharp on Saturday night. Don't be late."

With that, she stands and picks up her Nacho Surprise–laden tray.

"Oh," says Sami. "By the way, my dress is turquoise. In case you want to get me a corsage that matches." And she trots away.

"Wow. Oh wow. Oh wow," sputters Peanut.

"That did not just happen!" says Tater Tot.

"Of course it happened," says Drumstick. "My best buddy is a chick magnet! Trust me, I'm a rooster. I'm an expert on chicks."

"Sweet!" says Sea-Monkey. "Give me five up top!"

But I do not give him five up top. I sit there in silence. Contemplating the universe and its many mysteries.

"You okay, dude?" Darvish asks after a moment.

"Darvish, I have just unraveled a riddle that crosses the physical and the spiritual planes of existence. I have played a game of chance against Death himself and lived to tell the tale. I am friend to rhinos and companion of sharks. Of course I'm okay."

"All right, all right."

"There is just one question that plagues me," I say. "One question that lingers on the fringe of my already overtaxed mind."

"Yeah?"

"What on earth is a corsage?"

26

I may have blacked out over lunch.

Darvish was kind enough to fill me in on the murkier details. Apparently, I am going to the Evening of Enchantment dance. With Sami Mulpepper.

The day has been a roller coaster of victorious elation and unsettling confusion. And yet, out of all the mysteries that this fathomless universe holds, I find myself in the midst of the most confounding of them all.

Gym class.

Let's be clear about something. I have assets, both numerous and plentiful.

I can name every breed of dog known to man.

Despite what you may have heard from others, I am mature beyond my years.

My rugged good looks are really something special.

However, you'll note that I did not list dodgeball skills among my assets.

That is because they are nonexistent. Until today.

Today, I cannot miss.

Today, I am king of the dodgeball court.

Today, the guys want to be me and the ladies want to be with me.

It is because I have a secret weapon.

Is my secret weapon some heretofore untapped reserve of athletic talent? No.

Is my secret weapon my upbeat attitude in the face of adversity? Not really.

Is my secret weapon the disequilibrium that comes from being unexpectedly invited to a social gathering by a girl? Not even close.

My secret weapon is this: I have four invisible friends on the court. Five, if you count the shark. They are making the ball go where I want it to go. And they are having the time of their lives . . . umm . . . deaths.

I rocket the ball once again. Really more of a catapult than a rocket. Actually, more of a slingshot than a catapult. But no matter. Peanut bounces it off his box-shaped behind and nails Jason Kramer right in the noggin. Jason yowls in pain and staggers to the bleachers.

Tater Tot guards the other side of the court. "Sheesh, Rex! I'm wide open!" she screams. "Send the next one my way!"

Sea-Monkey is standing directly beside me defending my flanks. This may explain why I have not been hit once. He is also telling me a story about how, one time, chimps threw 370 different handfuls of chimp poo at him, and he dodged them all without even moving. I am really warming up to this gorilla.

Drumstick is running around like a maniac, screaming "KAMIKAZE!" and tripping people.

"How did you get so good at sports all of a sudden?" asks Darvish. It seems that nobody is aware of my dodgeball support crew. I guess people see what they want to see. To the mortal eye, I just look really skilled. I could get used to this.

"Let's just say I have a little help from the great beyond," I whisper to my best friend.

Darvish ducks a stray ball by diving into my protected aura. "That's cheating, Rex! You can't have dead animals help you win at dodgeball. It's against the rules!"

I'd like to see where that's written in the rule book. "What are you complaining about?" I yell. "We're actually winning for once!"

I am crazed with victory. Berserk with power. A ball ricochets off Sea-Monkey's chest and bounces harmlessly toward me. I grab the ball and fling it with the force of a bazooka.

My ball is way off course. But this hardly matters. Tater Tot head-butts it right at Holly Creskin. It hits her smack-dab in her big fat PUPAE button.

And that's when it hits me. Not the ball. But inspiration.

I turn to Darvish. "We need to know who would want to kill endangered species, right?"

"Not necessarily," he says. "If we never solve this, they could stick around and help us win the Dodgeball World Championships."

The kid has had worse ideas. "We'll call that Plan B," I say. "In the meantime, we need to know who is trying to wipe them out, right?"

"Yes," he agrees. "We need to know that."

"So, who are the enemies of endangered species?" I ask.

"I dunno."

"Exactly!" I say. "So, who *would* know?"

"I dunno."

"A group committed to protecting endangered species, that's who."

"I already took a ball to the head once today," he says, narrowly avoiding a well-aimed throw. "Are you trying to make my brain hurt worse?"

"I know where we can get more info," I say. I look at Holly Creskin limping off the court. Darvish follows my gaze.

"It's time to go to a PUPAE meeting."

"KAMIKAZE!!!" The other team captain trips on Drumstick and thuds to the ground, legs akimbo.

It warms the heart. It really does.

27

If only my rhino were as good at paying attention as she is at head-butting dodgeballs. She might have seen her attacker at the zoo.

If only my gorilla were as good at staying in his cage as he is at blocking errant projectiles. He might be safe at home rather than dead with a shark attached to his booty.

If only my elephant were as good at moving on to the afterlife as he is at being square. He might be in Peanut Paradise instead of following me around.

But they are not.

Which is why they need me.

Which is why I find myself spending Tuesday night at the Wombat Lodge, attending a meeting of

People United to Protect Animals Everywhere. One thousand members strong.

These folks have quite a recruiting strategy. I don't know what it is. But I am pretty sure it does not involve giving out cookies and punch at their meetings. Because I am currently cookieless. And punchless. Which is not a great recruiting strategy, but seems to be working for them.

Holly was only too happy to bring me and Darvish to her PUPAE meeting. It probably has to do with my newfound dodgeball prowess. Or those rugged good looks I mentioned before.

Except that Darvish has chickened out. I called him multiple times this afternoon.

No answer. Why he even has a cell phone is anybody's guess. After the fourteenth call, he texted me back. He claims that he had to go visit his Nani at her nursing home tonight.

It is an unlikely story. He has clearly cloaked his chickenheartedness in concern for the elderly. But I know the truth.

He is scared of Holly Creskin.

After school, I suggested to Darvish that he invite somebody to the dance. Perhaps Holly Creskin, as an example. Then he would not have to sit at home by himself like some sort of sad sack on the night in question. Also, I would have my sidekick close at hand in case things get weird with Sami Mulpepper. As I imagine they might. I do not know what happens at dances, but I suspect it may involve dancing.

Darvish did not like my suggestion.

I understand his misgivings. Holly Creskin is extremely girly, even for a girl. She wears too much perfume. And she has an unhealthy obsession with unicorns. However, in spite of my Darvishlessness, I am committed to my dead four-legged friends. So, I am now sitting at a PUPAE meeting side by side with Holly Creskin, the unicorn lover. Trying to listen to Talon Smithfield.

"See? I told you he was tall," she reminds me for the twelfth time tonight.

While I have encountered Talon Smithfield before at Buy-Buy Plaza, I confess I never paid him much attention. I examine him properly now. He is slightly above average in height. Perhaps I am misunderstanding Holly Creskin. Perhaps *tall* is her code word for *dreamy*. In which case, yes, I cannot deny that his crystal-blue eyes are rather bewitching.

"He's so passionate about the plight of wildlife," she whispers. "I just love that."

"Quiet," I whisper. "I'm trying to listen to your boyfriend."

Holly Creskin dissolves into hushed giggles, which allows me to focus on the task at hand.

Talon Smithfield, tall, crystal-eyed high schooler, presides over this meeting. From his position up front, he holds aloft some sort of sale flyer.

"For our final piece of business, I have sad news," he says. "Weird Bubba's Snakeskin Emporium has once more started selling pajamas made from snakes."

"Gasp!" gasp the PUPAE people.

"You may well gasp, as it is shocking," he says. "So, let's limit our pajama purchases there and show Weird Bubba and others like him that we are PUPAE! And we mean business!"

"Hooray!" shout the PUPAE people.

Talon lowers the flyer and looks around. "And that concludes our meeting for this month. Does anyone have any questions?"

My moment has come. I raise my hand.

"Yes, the little kid in the back," he says, pointing to me.

Little kid? I stand on my chair in a large and intimidating manner for reasons that should be obvious to you by now. "What about the animals that are being killed at the zoo?" I shout.

Talon shakes his head and takes a deep, shuddering breath. He is clearly distraught by this topic. It's understandable. He is king of the tree-huggers and animal-lovers. The deaths at the zoo must be taking a terrible toll on his tender heart. "Yes, that's definitely a horrible set of horribleness. It's just horrible and terrible and horrible." He wrings his hands in distress.

Great. I've rendered him unable to construct a cohesive sentence. But I am relentless in my pursuit of truth, justice, and the American Way. I probe further. "Yes, it's horrible. And terrible. Also, horrible again. But what does PUPAE know about it?"

Talon Smithfield stands tall and puts on a brave face. "The official stance of PUPAE is that we are very much against those animal deaths."

"Hooray!" shout the PUPAE people.

"But what if they're not just deaths?" I probe. "What if they are murders?"

He blanches at the thought.

"Who might be guilty of such a horrible, terrible, and horrible thing?" I ask.

He starts pacing anxiously. I have plainly upset his delicate constitution. "Probably not Weird Bubba," he says. "More than likely, it is some evil corporation. Or some other sinister people. I hate to speculate. But whoever it is, we are against them."

"Hooray!" shout the PUPAE people.

But if I'm going to get to the bottom of this, I need this guy to speculate whether he hates to or not. "But WHO?" I shout. "Who would be killing endangered species?"

Talon Smithfield looks around, like it's a secret

that he's not sure he wants to share. But then he steps forward and says it. "My money is on CES."

"CES?" shout the PUPAE people.

"Cageless Enclosure Solutions," clarifies Talon Smithfield. "A company led by this woman."

He holds up a CES pamphlet with a picture of a middle-aged woman. "Her name is Haughtry Vain. Her company is negotiating with the zoo to renovate all the animal cages in the entire zoo into open-air enclosures."

"Open-air enclosures," I say. "Isn't that a good thing?"

"A good thing?" says Talon Smithfield. "Enclosed animals are never a good thing."

"Yeah!" shout the PUPAE people.

"If this deal with Middling Zoo goes through, CES will make millions of dollars on the zoo renovation. At the animals' expense!"

"That's exploitation!" cries Holly Creskin.

"Indeed, it is, Miss Creskin," says Talon Smithfield. "If CES had their way, every endangered species in the world would live in one of their expensive open-air enclosures. We believe that the best animal enclosure is the wild."

"Hooray!" shout the PUPAE people.

"Hooray is right," says Talon Smithfield. "These animal deaths seem to be just the thing to make the zoo move forward with this deal. So, who stands to gain by these animal deaths? Cageless Enclosure Solutions, that's who! And we at PUPAE do not support CES and their greedy corporate agenda!"

"Hooray!" shout the PUPAE people.

Bingo, I shout inside my head. It's all coming together.

"So keep recruiting, people!" he says. "And I'll see you at next month's meeting."

I lean over to Peanut, who is wedged into four empty seats behind me. With no Darvish to accompany me, I recruited Peanut for moral support.

"The person you saw in the shadows. The one that opened your cage. Could it have been that woman? Could it have been Haughtry Vain?"

"Oh gee whiz," he says. "So hard to say. It was so dark. And I was distracted by the peanuts."

So far, Peanut is failing in his task to support me morally.

But the evening is not wasted. We have a clear suspect. Haughtry Vain. Even her name sounds sinister. If we can somehow prove that she is behind this litany of carnage, my dead pet squad is home free.

Most of the PUPAE members are clearing out. I am still cookieless. Which is an affront to humanity, not to mention my stomach. I linger toward the front in the hopes of finding an undiscovered snack tray.

"That is the one," says a soft voice.

I shiver with an unexpected chill and turn around. I am face-to-face with a panda. Its fur stands on end like it lost a fight with an electrical socket. Ghastly green ghost vapor rolls to the floor around it. It sits casually in a folding chair. Chewing on a cookie.

This is getting out of hand. Another dead animal. And what's even worse, the panda has a cookie and I don't.

"What did you say?" I ask it.

"That is the one," she says again, pointing. "That is the human who killed me."

I turn around, following the panda's accusing paw. She is pointing at the picture of Haughtry Vain. Talon

Smithfield is holding it up between himself and Holly Creskin. No doubt using it as a shield against Holly's shameless flirtatious advances.

I turn back to the panda before me. She is cute beyond all reason. And yet, despite her fuzzy-wuzzy adorableness, a harsh realization hits me afresh. This panda bear is dead. Yet one more victim to appear before me, robbed of life. I feel my heart sink. Perhaps the plight of these poor creatures is beginning to make my own heart as tender and mushy as Talon Smithfield's.

And yet, despite my mushy heart, I can't help but feel a surge of victory coursing through me. For this panda has been able to do what a rhino, gorilla, and elephant have been unable to do before her. Identify her killer.

Yet something remains unanswered. The one question that could be the key to everything. The riddle that could unlock so much. And only I am brave enough to ask it.

I lean in close to the panda. And I boldly ask the question that needs asking.

"Where'd you get the cookie?"

28

It seems that lately, every time I return to my bedroom, I have another dearly departed zoo animal in tow.

Only tonight when I return, the other deceased animals and the deceased barnyard bird are giving each other manicures with nail polish they have pilfered from my mom.

Which does not happen every time I return to my bedroom. Nor should it.

"Can I come in?" I ask.

"It's your room," says Tater Tot.

"Well, I don't want to disturb whatever you call this."

"We call it spa night!" says Drumstick.

"Oh, how fun!" says Peanut, joining the merriment.

"It was the chicken's idea," says Sea-Monkey.

"We've got to pass the time somehow," squawks Drumstick. "Eternity is a long time!"

"I had my doubts," says the gorilla. "But this is really quite relaxing." His nails are Sea Glass Green. Which, I must admit, brings out his eyes. He munches on chocolate truffles. Also pilfered from my mother.

On the drive home, the panda spilled the beans on her recent demise. Listening to the horrors of this encounter in the backseat of the Creskin-mobile without tipping off Holly Creskin or her mother was no easy feat, let me tell you. But I'm learning to mask my emotions to the mortals around me behind a facade of cool detachment.

The panda's story is this: Earlier this evening, somebody opened her cage. That same somebody released her from her cage. She was then attacked by that selfsame somebody—with a Taser—which accounts for her high-voltage hairdo and her current less-than-alive status.

I close my bedroom door and teleconference Darvish in. Which, to the layperson, means I call him on the phone. He's not supposed to have calls after 9:00 p.m., but this is mission-critical.

"What's going on, Rex?" he grumbles. "You know I can't have calls this late."

"You are on speakerphone, Darvish," I inform him. "And I should preface this Meeting of the Minds by clarifying that there is a dead panda in our midst."

"A panda?" he groans. "Why am I not surprised? And the correct term is Spirit Summit."

"You should also be advised that my room is currently a nail salon."

"Spa," corrects Tater Tot. "It's obviously a spa."

"Why are you calling me, Rex?" Darvish whines. "I'm going to get in trouble."

"If you hadn't been off gallivanting with your Nani, you would know," I tell him.

"We weren't gallivanting. She's ninety-two. She doesn't gallivant."

"Try to stay on topic, Darvish," I say. "Clearly, the circumstances are dire or I wouldn't be calling. Dire circumstances overrule your parents' arbitrary rules. I don't mean to be rude, but this is the way the world works. The sooner you come to terms with it, the better."

Darvish sighs in defeat. "What is it?"

I turn to the panda. "Tell them."

The panda looks around the room. "I know who killed us."

"Holy crud!" says Drumstick.

"Holy crud!" says Tater Tot.

"Holy crud!" says Sea-Monkey.

"Holy crud!" says Peanut.

"Mfwolymwud!" says the shark.

"Holy crud indeed," I confirm.

"What's going on?" Darvish's voice crackles with exasperation. "You know I can't hear them!"

"Oh, sorry." I keep doing that. Associating with the spiritually unattuned can be burdensome at times. "The panda knows who killed her."

"Her who?"

"Her the panda."

"Are you sure?"

"She identified the killer," I say. I look to the panda

for support, but she is wrapped up in the task of picking a new nail color. She's had a rough day. Maybe a manicure is just the thing to lift her spirits.

I turn back to the phone and whisper to Darvish. "It's some person named Haughtry Vain."

"Holy crud!" says Darvish.

"Holy crud indeed," I confirm.

"The president of CES?" he says.

"How do you know about Cageless Enclosure Solutions?"

"I read, Rex," he says. "It makes total sense! They are working with the zoo. Remember that article of mine you read for current events?"

"I remember reading an article," I say. "However, if I recall correctly, the exact ownership of the article was up for debate."

"Whatever. It said Haughtry Vain is a consultant for the zoo! Which means that she has zoo access."

The kid is onto something. "I hate to admit it, but you're right," I say. "Haughtry Vain had both motive and access."

"Why do you hate to admit it?" he asks. "I'm right at least seventy-five percent of the time."

I don't have time to coddle Darvish's ego right now. There is an electri-fried panda with Passionfruit Pink nails tugging on my sleeve. The service in this spa is exceptional.

"We must stop the killer, Rex," the panda says. "Kou Kou could be next."

"She says Kou Kou could be next," I say.

"She who?"

"She the panda!" I shout. "Do your level best to concentrate, Darvish."

I turn back to the panda. "Who's Kou Kou?"

"The other panda," answers Darvish. "I just looked it up on the Internet. Mei Mei and Kou Kou are the two giant pandas at the zoo. And, Rex . . ."

"What?"

"If it's Mei Mei that's with you . . ."

"It's the girl one."

"How do you know that?"

"Because she's wearing a skirt."

"Really?"

This kid. "No, Darvish! Not really! It's obviously because she has a girl's voice. Try to keep up, son."

"Right," he says. "Then that means Kou Kou is the last one."

"The last what?"

"The last endangered species at the Middling Zoo."

A hush settles over the crowd. Nail-polish brushes freeze mid-stroke.

"That clinches it!" says Sea-Monkey. "This could be our last chance to properly pummel whoever's doing this!" He blows on his nails.

"You're right," I say.

"I told you, I'm right like seventy-five percent of the time," says Darvish.

"Not you," I clarify. "Sea-Monkey."

"Right about what? I CAN'T HEAR THEM!"

I stand on my bed in triumph. "We're going to infiltrate the Middling Zoo!" I proclaim. "We'll save Kou Kou and catch the culprit once and for all!"

"What about the pudgy guard?" Darvish sounds worried.

"We'll cross that bridge when we come to it!" I say. "We have a panda to save!"

It's the perfect plan. Detailed. Thorough. Astute. Nothing can go wrong.

"Hooray!" cheers Drumstick. "Another field trip to the zoo!"

The chicken jumps into the air, spilling Ooh-La-La Orange all over my pillow.

I shake my head in frustration. This is why I can't have nice things.

29

Turns out, you cannot flush a pillow down the toilet.

"It's not technically my fault," I say.

"What are you doing?!" my dad asks, sloshing through the ankle-deep water.

Being responsible, that's what.

First, I knew my parents would be emotionally agitated at the sight of a nail-polish stain on my furniture. Getting rid of the offending pillow saves them pain and suffering. Win.

Second, I would have had to explain the presence of said nail-polish stain. I am running out of good cover-up stories. This might have led to the discovery of my ghostly houseguests. Nobody benefits from that. So I took responsibility for my steamrolled chicken's buffoonery and attempted to dispose of the evidence. Win-win.

Plus, if the pillow is in our septic system instead of in my room, my dad does not have to launder it. Win-win-win.

Except there is a small hiccup that nobody, and I mean nobody, could have foreseen. Turns out, you cannot flush a pillow down the toilet.

My dad is doing some deep-breathing exercises, which seems counterproductive to the present predicament. Mopping would be far more helpful.

"Don't blame yourself," I tell him comfortingly.

"What?!"

"It's true. We would not be in this situation if you had sprung for better plumbing instead of these chintzy low-capacity pipes we have."

"Please get out of here," he says. Tears fill his eyes.

Poor guy. He can be so hard on himself. "Never skimp when it comes to plumbing." I offer these parting nuggets of wisdom to encourage him as I take my leave. These are words to live by. I can see by the throbbing vein in his forehead that he knows it.

It is the kind of forward thinking that I try to imbue my life with. The sort of well-thought-out reasoning that dooms my zoo infiltration plan to glorious success.

30

Villains come in all shapes and sizes.

Some have mechanical octopus arms.

Some were burnt by acid as children and now wear clown makeup to compensate.

And some are missing half their heads.

Haughtry Vain is the latter. Darvish has printed off a picture of Haughtry Vain from the Internet. He brought it to school today. She should fire her photographer. Because her picture looks like this:

As you can see, she is very capable of the travesties of which she is accused. Anybody with pixels covering half their face like that would be likely to lash out at the world.

"My printer was running out of ink," says Darvish. "That's why it looks like that."

Haughtry Vain can blame it on Darvish's printer all she likes, but it's quite clear: This woman is capable of anything.

"I still don't understand," Darvish says. "Exactly how are we supposed to catch her?"

I breathe the exasperated sigh of the eternally patient.

"It's easy," I explain. "We go to the zoo after school today. We hide somewhere until after closing. We catch the villain in the act, expose her misdeeds, and emerge victorious."

I sometimes forget that the obvious needs to be spelled out to people. If I have a flaw, it's that.

"But HOW exactly are we going to catch her?" he persists. "After we hide, what are we going to DO?"

"We'll wing it." It's the perfect plan. I still don't see why he can't get on board.

"But what if somebody catches us in the zoo after hours?"

"Don't worry, Darvish," I assure him. "I have Fists of Furry to protect us."

"Don't you mean Fists of Fury?"

"First, do you want to be on the receiving end of Fists of Furry?"

"No."

"I don't want that either," I tell him. "So please

stop contradicting me. Second, I am talking about gorilla fists. And they are furry. So, when I say Fists of Furry, rest assured that I mean what I say."

But Darvish has spotted another "hole" in what is otherwise a foolproof stratagem.

"I'm not allowed to stay out that late," he protests.

"Well, don't tell your parents that's what you're doing," I say. "You tell them you're sleeping at my house. Which you'll do. After we emerge victorious. So, it's not a lie."

I have a lot of work to do still, molding my sidekick. He doesn't seem to grasp that dire situations will always trump rules and regulations.

"By the way," I say, "your idea to invite Holly Creskin to the Evening of Enchantment Dance may be ill-advised."

"What??" Darvish sputters. "That wasn't my idea. It was yours!"

"There's no need to quibble on the details, Darvish. I know heartbreak is hard. But you should try to put her from your mind."

He rolls his eyes to the heavens. "What are you talking about?"

I decide to let him down easy. "There is a high schooler named Talon Smithfield who is vying for her affections. He is tall. And dreamy. And has crystalline eyes that are the steely blue of an iceberg on a crisp December night. You cannot hope to compete with that."

"I'm not trying to compete!" he hisses. "I don't like Holly Creskin!"

"That's the spirit," I say, patting him on the arm.

Ms. Yardley clears her throat loudly. "Perhaps you two would like to join the rest of the class in listening to Jason's report," she says. "Unless you'd enjoy another recess detention."

Here's another one who seems to have no perspective of the grand design. Ms. Yardley does not recognize a Meeting of the Minds in session right under her nose. She should be proud that we have chosen her classroom to put together our plan to infiltrate the zoo. Historic far-reaching events are unfolding before her and she is missing out.

Would she have scolded Abraham Lincoln for writing the Declaration of Independence during Jason Kramer's oral report?

Would she have stopped Christopher Columbus from discovering Antarctica if he happened to be doing it in her classroom?

Would she have lectured Willy Wonka for inventing the Evershrinking Blobgobber just because it interfered with her lesson plan?

Sadly, the answer is probably a resounding yes. Ms. Yardley appreciates the heck out of a good fraction, but, sadly, she has no respect for cosmic contributions to history.

I sigh and give my attention to the pointless report coming from Jason Kramer's face. I feel a momentary pang of jealousy for Abraham Lincoln, Christopher Columbus, and Willy Wonka. They had no idea of the hardships with which I grapple on a daily basis.

31

"Get your knee out of my nose," says Darvish.

Spending three hours crammed into the bottom of a snow cone stand is never pleasant. It is doubly so when you are crammed in there with your best friend and a dead chicken, a dead rhino, a dead gorilla, a dead shark, a dead elephant, and a dead panda.

That's a whole lot of dead in a very small space. But it is for the greater good, so I endure.

"Count yourself lucky," I tell Darvish. "At least you don't have a big fat rhino knee in your face."

"You better watch it with that fat talk," she says. "I move my horn three inches to the right and you're walking bowlegged for the next ten years."

"They're in here with us?" Darvish asks. "I don't feel them."

"Apparently, it's just another one of the joys of being me," I tell him.

"Why didn't you have them wait outside?" he says. "Nobody can see them or feel them except you!"

It is a valid point. It would have been nice if he had brought it up earlier. But the zoo has been closed for three hours now, so I deem it safe to emerge from our hiding place. I open the latch to the snow cone stand and we tumble out in a heap of legs, arms, trunks, horns, and beaks.

I attempt to free myself from the fray, but my foot catches on the snow cone banner. The enormous banner rips free from the stand and entangles us in its canvas clutches.

We are one smooth operation, let me tell you.

At this less than opportune moment, I hear footsteps. Everyone freezes.

"It's the gnome guard!" hisses Darvish.

"Hobbit guard," I correct him. "Gnomes are a totally different thing." How he could mix up his mythological creatures at a critical moment such as this is beyond me.

"Whatever!" he whispers. "The guard is coming! Nobody move!"

We freeze in a huddled heap. Through the trees I see the shadows of the guard. My portly friend rolls along, flashlight in hand.

The beam of his flashlight shines toward the roped-off rhino enclosure and pauses for a moment. Then the guard turns and heads in our direction.

I can see the whites of the guard's greedy little eyes as he leads his lackeys our way. I suspect he has his sights set on the possibility of free snow cones contained in our snow cone stand.

Suddenly, there are footfalls and low voices from the opposite side of us. Over by the Reptile House, I see it. More flashlights.

Sweet kiwi-lime snow cones! More guards! Through the darkness, I spy at least four figures, the beams of their lights scanning the grounds methodically. The zoo has clearly beefed up security in the wake of recent events.

I feel panic grip my chest. Either that or it's Darvish tightly hugging me. Either way, it's a horrific and helpless feeling.

Their paths will lead them to converge on our snow cone stand. And here we are, gift-wrapped and waiting for beardless Santa and his elves to deliver us to the zoo-trespassing authorities.

Here we are, rolled up like some weird Shire-made burrito, awaiting their hobbity appetites.

Here we are, swaddled like an exotic sushi roll of doom.

It's only a matter of seconds before their lights will fall directly on our pathetic bundle.

CRASH!

The sound shatters the quiet night. The moment I hear it, I assume it is my heart exploding in terror. But it's not. Something loud and metallic has smashed on the other side of the zoo, back near the entrance.

The guards have heard it, too. Their flashlights jerk away from us, toward the sound. The new guards see this opportunity to show their great worth, and they dash toward the zoo entrance with gusto, leaving my roly-poly nemesis eating their dust. The round one curses and starts toddling toward the entrance as quickly as his little legs will carry him.

We stay frozen.

We wait.

We listen.

And that's when Drumstick walks right up to me. He starts pulling at the banner with his beak, trying to untangle me.

"Where did you come from?" I ask him. "I thought you were wrapped up in here with us."

"I was," he clucks. "But when the guards started heading this way, I thought I'd better wiggle out and make a distraction."

I am nearly speechless. "You did that?"

He nods his head. "Trash can," he says.

I can't believe it. It is nothing short of brilliant. I have clearly underestimated the brainpower of chickens. "I could kiss you!" I say.

"Rain check," he says. "You guys need to get unwrapped before they come back."

He's right. After several minutes of struggle, which includes much cursing (that gorilla has a mouth on him) and the chicken running around screaming "BAKED POTATOES!" (don't ask me why; clearly his moment of brilliance has passed), we are free and ready for action.

"What's the plan?" asks Darvish.

"Kou Kou is Haughtry Vain's next target," I remind him. "So that's where we should be. Let's get over to the panda paddock and lie in wait."

"Are you sure they don't have security cameras?" he asks nervously.

"Are you kidding?" I ask. "If they hire Haughtry Vain and her band of thugs to renovate the zoo enclosures, it will cost them millions. They're saving their pennies."

"I hope you're right," Darvish says, creeping anxiously into the open. "Otherwise this whole plan is in the toilet."

"Have you ever known me not to be right?" I ask.

"I'm not going to answer that."

There is no sign of the guards. The zoo seems empty as we make our way to the Far East Pavilion. Exhibits and signs that are cheerful during the day cast long and creepy shadows in the darkness, like arms reaching out to snatch us. The occasional rumble or growl from the animal cages breaks the silence.

But when we arrive at Kou Kou's paddock, another problem rears its ugly head. The enclosure is a good twenty-five feet below the viewing rail where we stand. There's no way in.

"Now what?" says Darvish.

"There is a zookeeper entrance down below," says Mei Mei. "They use it to feed us. That is where the killer came in."

"The zookeeper entrance will be locked," I say. "And we don't have a key."

"That's true," says Darvish. He points. "Do you think we could shinny down those tall bamboo stalks?" I follow his gaze. There are tons of bamboo plants growing in the panda enclosure. Some of the stalks almost reach the top of the enclosure.

"Nope. Nope," Peanut says. "That bamboo looks splintery. There's no way I'm getting on that. Not for all the peanuts in China."

"Me neither," agrees Tater Tot.

I don't try to talk them into it. The bamboo is flimsy stuff. "I don't think it will hold our weight," I say.

"BAKED POTATOES!" squawks the chicken.

"Not helpful," I tell him.

"Yes, it is!" he says. "Follow me!" Drumstick takes off back the way we came.

I slap my palm to my forehead in frustration.

"Stay here," I tell Darvish. And, goodness knows why, I take off after the chicken. Perhaps his flash of ingenuity was a one-off, but I can't help feeling that he's got something up his flattened feathery sleeve.

But when I finally catch up with him, he's just standing and staring.

"BAKED POTATOES!" he screams again.

I look. There in front of us is a baked potato stand. It's a lot like the snow cone stand where we hid earlier, but much bigger. Which is not helpful. But then I take a closer look.

"My lightning reflexes and quick thinking are clearly rubbing off on you," I tell the bird.

"Okay," he says.

When I run back to Darvish, I'm dragging a long yellow canvas.

"What's that?" asks Darvish.

I tie the end of the canvas to the railing and throw

the rest down into the panda paddock. It falls all the way to the bottom. But as the thirty-foot banner falls, it unfurls, showing everyone what is written on it.

"BAKED POTATOES!" Drumstick and I squawk together.

32

Sometimes accomplishing lofty deeds just takes the right tool for the right job.

Sherlock Holmes's tool was a magnifying glass. It helped him solve crime.

Benjamin Franklin had that kite. It helped him invent lightning.

Dora the Explorer had a singing backpack. It helped her entertain small children in an annoying way.

In my case, the right tool happens to be an enormous baked potato sign. And the right job is getting into an enclosure containing a giant endangered panda.

Which is where Darvish and I are now.

If you ever find yourself needing to slide down

a baked potato banner into a panda enclosure at the zoo, there are three things that you need to know.

1. Sliding down a baked potato banner into a panda enclosure is a cinch. Any numbskull can do it.
2. Climbing up a baked potato banner out of a panda enclosure is not quite as easy.
3. One of the side effects of climbing into a panda enclosure with no way out is that you find yourself trapped face-to-face with an angry panda.

Which is where we are now. Kou Kou is large. He is wide. He is lonely. And he looks very cranky to find us here.

"What now, Mr. Wing-It?" asks Darvish, grabbing on to me.

"Mei Mei?" I look around. But the panda, elephant, gorilla, and rhino are nowhere to be found. Even the chicken is gone.

Great. Just like a ghost to get ashes all over your beanbag chair, get nail polish all over your pillow, and then split when things get real.

"Nice Kou Kou," I say, backing away. I really hope I'm pronouncing his name right. The only thing that could make this situation worse is an offended panda.

"Pandas don't eat people, right?" asks Darvish, as he hides behind me. "I thought they only ate plants. Like bamboo and stuff."

"I can't be expected to know everything, Darvish!" I say, backing up still farther. "You're the one who reads, remember?"

I feel the wall of bamboo plants against my back and know we've run out of room. And that's when I feel something grab my foot.

"AAAHHH!" I scream. It's worth noting that my scream is not the terrified scream of a little child lost in a bamboo forest being set upon by a black-and-white creature from the Far East. It is simply the surprised scream of a man of the world finding that something has had the chutzpah to grab his manly foot.

"AAAHHH!" Darvish screams, too. His scream is the little lost child scream I was talking about earlier. It lacks any form of chutzpah.

I look down and see that the hand on my foot is not really a hand. It is a paw. A black-and-white paw. With the fur standing up on end.

It is Mei Mei. Tater Tot and the others lurk in the bamboo behind her.

She is pointing to some type of weird flower pod in the brush.

"Lantern blossom pod," she says softly.

"That's not going to fill him up!" I yell. "He'll still have plenty of room left to eat Darvish."

"What?!" screams Darvish, panic-stricken. "Who's eating me?"

But Mei Mei ignores me as she emerges from the bamboo, toward Kou Kou. And she begins doing something she's never done before.

Mei Mei glows.

Not her normal glimmer of green vapor. She is shining with a radiant golden light. And the strange thing is . . . Kou Kou seems to see her.

"Lantern blossom pods are quite rare," she whispers. "Together, we have found them here on two other occasions. Give it to Kou Kou. He knows I am here with you."

This flower-power plan sounds very untrustworthy to me. But I am out of options. So even though I'm convinced that Darvish and I are about to be panda chow, I take the strange pod. It is round and springy, about the size and weight of a soccer ball. I reach out and lay it at the feet of the advancing Kou Kou.

Kou Kou stops. He looks at the lantern blossom pod. He looks back toward Mei Mei. A new expression comes over his face.

Less grumpy. More sad.

Less angry. More lonely.

He sniffs the lantern blossom. He gently nudges it back toward Mei Mei, like some sort of offering. Then he slowly lumbers toward the back of his paddock.

I breathe a sigh of relief. Possibly my first breath in several minutes.

I look at Darvish. "Why didn't you think of that?"

33

There's not even time for Darvish to make a witty comeback. Because suddenly we hear a metallic click and a creak coming from the back wall of the enclosure.

"That's the cage being opened," says Mei Mei.

"Yep. Yep." Peanut nods his head. "That's just what it sounded like. That's definitely the sound of the cage door."

"Oh, yeah. I definitely remember that sound," says Tater Tot. "It still sends a shiver up my spine."

"You think that's a scary sound?" says Sea-Monkey. "That's nothing! One time I accidentally ate a whole pile of ghost-gas fungus. Every time I went to the bathroom, it sounded like my butt was haunted. *That* was a scary sound!"

I turn to Darvish. "That's the cage being opened," I tell him.

"How do you know?" he asks.

"I just know things," I say. "It's best not to question my intuition."

Peanut covers his face. "Oh gosh. I hope there are no peanuts this time. I'm just not myself when peanuts are involved."

We dive into the bamboo and hide, which is a tight squeeze for two kids, four large zoo mammals, a shark, and a chicken. But we manage.

Now that my eyes have adjusted to the dark, I see there is a door along the back wall, painted to blend in to the bamboo. But right now, it stands open. There is a light coming from it.

The beam of a flashlight.

"This is what happened before," says Mei Mei. "But last time I wandered out the door and the human was waiting for me."

"Then we need to make sure Kou Kou doesn't do that," I say.

"Leave that to me," she says and shambles back to Kou Kou. I watch as her glowing form dissolves into some sort of mist. The glowing gold cloud floats toward Kou Kou and surrounds his head. He closes his eyes and seems to breathe it in through his nose. A look of peace covers his face.

I have witnessed something very special.

I have witnessed something very momentous.

I have witnessed something very disgusting. I had no idea that these guys could turn into some sort of snot-mist and go inside my breathy holes. I'm just thankful none of them have tried it on me.

But I can see that Kou Kou isn't going to wander out the door. Which means Haughtry Vain will have to come inside for him.

I whisper to Darvish. "We need to set some kind of trap to capture Haughtry Vain when she comes in."

"No time," he says, trembling beside me. "Here she comes."

He's right. A figure enters through the door.

It is the sinister Haughtry Vain. She shines the sinister flashlight in her sinister hand around the paddock. It hits the wall. The floor. The bamboo. And then lands right on my face.

If you ever find yourself hiding in a panda paddock, don't use the bamboo as a hiding place. It may be too thin to successfully hide behind. More research is warranted.

But from the spill of the flashlight, I can see her features. And realize a couple other important details.

Haughtry Vain is taller than I expected.

She is younger than I expected.

She has much dreamier eyes than I expected.

And she looks exactly like Talon Smithfield.

34

My powers of deductive reasoning have somehow failed me. My intuitive perception has, inexplicably, led me astray. My nimble mind has, against all odds, tripped on its own feet.

I don't know how, but I suspect Darvish is to blame.

"Hey!" says Talon Smithfield. "You're the little kid from the PUPAE meeting! What are you doing here?"

Little kid? This guy's villainy knows no bounds.

"That's the knucklehead who opened my cage," whispers Sea-Monkey. "I recognize his aftershave. Smells like sandalwood and something else."

"Death," says Peanut.

"Yep. That's it," confirms Tater Tot. "Sandalwood and death."

Darvish grabs me by the shirt and shakes me. "I thought Mei Mei said it was Haughtry Vain!" he whispers tersely.

"I'm a victim of false testimony," I mutter back. "She pointed right at Haughtry's picture."

"Was Talon Smithfield holding the picture at the time?"

"I don't remember, on the grounds that it might incriminate me."

"You dummy!" hisses Darvish. "She was pointing at him!"

"It's not technically my fault!" I clarify. "Her paws are like oven mitts. She should be more specific with her fluffy-handed pointing."

But our Meeting of the Minds is cut short.

"Hey!" says Talon Smithfield. He clicks something in his hand and the blue sparks of a Taser zap to life. "What are you kids doing here?"

But it doesn't matter whether he's Haughtry Vain or Talon Smithfield or the Queen of England for that matter. He will fall victim to my devious coercion. For I have come up with an inspired plan. It is a plan even Her Royal Majesty would be fooled by.

I call it the "Play Along" Plan.

"I'm here to help you," I say, with a big, sinister grin on my face. "To rid the world of these annoying endangered species once and for all."

It is pure brilliance on my part. A plan of epic proportions that cannot fail.

"Nice try," he says. "Come out of that bamboo."

Except that it fails. Which is something that nobody, and I mean nobody, could have anticipated. This Talon Smithfield is a diabolical genius with more ingenuity than I have given him credit for.

"Come out of there." He brandishes his Taser in our direction. Darvish and I emerge from the scrub. "Oh, I see you brought a little friend with you."

"I'm not that little," says Darvish.

"Don't let him get inside your head," I advise Darvish. "It's just a ploy he uses to manipulate the weak-minded. Don't fall victim to his wily ways and dreamboat eyes."

Talon Smithfield clicks the Taser, making it spark with electricity. "I suppose you little tree-huggers are here to stop me."

Darvish stuffs his hands in his pockets. "You're Talon Smithfield," he says. Poor kid. He's resorted to stating the obvious.

"That's right," says Talon. "So what?"

"So, you're the president of PUPAE," says Darvish. "Aren't you supposed to be king of the tree-huggers?"

"Give me a break," he says. "I don't care about animals. I created PUPAE because stuff like that looks really great on college applications."

"He's right," agrees Darvish, nodding at me. "University admissions committees love community involvement."

"Starting PUPAE was easy. You don't have to do anything. You just have to be against stuff. Be against snakeskin pajamas. Be against using bunny rabbits as crash dummies. Be against scarecrows, which seriously traumatize poor defenseless crows."

"Sounds easy enough," says Darvish. "Any dimwit can be against something."

"Yeah, but nobody wanted to join!" says Talon, scowling. "Colleges don't care if you're the president of a group with no members!"

"So you took action," says Darvish. "By killing the Sumatran rhino."

Darvish is pacing now. He's warming up. He's fallen into the classic blunder . . . trying to reason with your culprit. But it is clear that words are useless to our current predicament.

"I didn't mean to kill it," says Talon.

"Did he just call me an 'it'?" snorts Tater Tot. "That guy is pure evil. And, I gotta say, super dashing for a human."

"It's those piercing sapphire eyes that really get you," I whisper.

"You're not wrong."

Talon Smithfield rolls his piercing sapphire eyes

disdainfully at Darvish. "I was trying to free that stupid rhino, not kill it," he explains.

"Why would you free it?" asks Darvish.

"I thought if an endangered species escaped, if I returned it to its natural habitat, then people would get excited about PUPAE."

He's making a classic blunder. Everyone knows that Middling Falls isn't a rhino's natural habitat. It barely qualifies as a human's natural habitat.

"Sure, sure," says Darvish. "Freeing it with fire. Makes total sense."

"Be quiet!" growls Talon Smithfield. "I was trying to drive it out of its pen with the fire. So it would run away. But the fire kind of got out of control." Talon even looks a little apologetic as he says it.

"*Kind of* got out of control?" cries Tater Tot. "Sheesh! Would you look at me! I'm a charcoal briquette!"

"Please," says Sea-Monkey. "You call that a burn? That's nothing! I once died in a forest fire with third-degree burns over a hundred and seventy-five percent of my body! I resuscitated myself using only a bullfrog and an electric eel and grew all new skin!"

It is good Darvish can't hear the gorilla. Because that kid will believe anything, and even I'm having a hard time believing this one. I mean, where is a gorilla going to get an electric eel?

"But people signed up for PUPAE," Darvish says to Talon Smithfield.

"Like crazy!" Talon Smithfield nods. "It worked. For some reason, people really cared about that endangered rhino. And that's when I realized I had a gold mine on my hands!"

"Hey, yeah!" I say. "You're charging people fifty-nine ninety-nine to be part of your made-up fake organization!"

He looks at me as if he's just realizing I'm standing there. "College is expensive! That's fifty-nine ninety-nine per membership that was going straight into my pocket! So I tried again with the gorilla. But that dumb monkey didn't escape. It just wandered into the Oceanarium and fell into the shark tank."

"Mwaafhaafhaa!" says the shark. "Fweejoostcaldjyooadummunkoo!"

"I know he just called me a dumb monkey!" growls Sea-Monkey at the shark. "My ears are at least a million times bigger than yours!" He turns to me. "Can you believe this guy?"

"And then even more people signed up!" says Darvish. "And you made even more money."

"Membership skyrocketed!"

"But something went wrong again with the elephant," says Darvish.

"I lured the elephant into a big truck with a trail of peanuts. It was the perfect plan. But it was late. I needed a coffee before I drove out to the country to release it. I parked the truck in the junkyard so nobody would find it. When I came back with my coffee, the truck was gone."

"I'm so sorry. Can he repeat that?" says Peanut indignantly. "Did he say 'gone'? While he was ordering a chai latte, that truck was getting crushed into a teeny box. With me and the peanuts inside it!"

"You killed three endangered animals!" I cry.

"Four, Rexxie," Drumstick reminds me. "Don't forget the panda."

"You killed four endangered animals!" I cry.

"It wasn't my fault!" Talon Smithfield says. "I never meant for them to die. Even the panda shouldn't have died. I just Tased it! I was just trying to subdue it. I didn't think it would kill it! It's not my fault that these animals are so frail and weak!"

"Wait a minute," Darvish cries. "How in the world did you get access to the zoo or the cages? PUPAE wouldn't have that kind of zoo access!"

Talon Smithfield laughs. "Brilliant, right?" he says. "I know the daughter of the zoo board president. She's in PUPAE! This dopey little grade-school girl is hopelessly in love with me. She'll do anything for me! Including steal her dad's key."

My heart plummets. The sound of crying unicorns and weeping rainbows fills my head. Because he's talking about Holly Creskin.

"With those keys, you can come and go as you please," says Darvish with realization.

"Why do you think the president of the zoo board is keeping it all under wraps?" crows Talon Smithfield. "Because he knows that his keys are being used! If it got out, he'd be ruined!"

He takes a step toward us. He no longer looks apologetic. For the first time, those crystal baby blues look dangerous.

"So . . . what am I going to do with you two?"

35

Darvish is all talk.

There he stands, hands in his pockets, chatting away with Talon Smithfield like it's their first date.

"I've got it!" says Talon Smithfield. "I'll tie you up! I'll video me rescuing this poor defenseless panda from the horrible murderers!"

"What murderers?" asks Darvish.

"You!" shouts Talon Smithfield. "I'll say I came to protect the panda."

"You can't do that!" cries Darvish.

"Of course I can! Nobody will believe a couple kids over the president of People United to Protect Animals Everywhere!"

This is where all of Darvish's talking has gotten us. Framed by a hunky teenager. Thanks to my best friend, we'll spend the prime of our lives rotting in the slammer. The clink. The big house.

Luckily, I am not all talk. Luckily, I am a man of action. And as such, I realize something that Darvish is incapable of realizing. Talking with this guy is useless. Guys like Talon Smithfield only understand brute force.

Muscle.

Brawn.

Action.

Clout.

Also, hair gel and teeth-whitening strips. Possibly colored contact lenses.

Unfortunately, Talon Smithfield is very large. It pains me to admit that he physically outclasses me by a mile. Plus, he has a Taser and I am blatantly Taserless.

But I possess something he never can.

A ridiculous amount of intuition.

An enormous knack for improvisation.

An uncanny flair for inspiration.

These things come with the territory when you're mature beyond your years.

"You'll get the blame," crows Talon Smithfield.

"And I'll be a hero. Colleges will love it! It's the perfect thing to do with you! This is working better than I expected. I'm so glad you kids showed up!"

I look Talon Smithfield square in the eyes. "I have a better idea of what you could do with us," I say. "Play dodgeball."

Talon squints at me. "What did you say, kid?"

Darvish squints at me. "What did you say, kid?"

I bend down and pick up the lantern blossom pod. Darvish grabs my arm. "What are you doing, dude?"

My eyes stay trained on Talon, but in my periphery, I can see the others. Tater Tot, Sea-Monkey, and Peanut have picked up my cue. They are in motion. Even Drumstick is moving into position.

"I'm going to do exactly what I said. Play dodgeball."

Talon clicks the Taser again, making sparks fly. "Don't try anything dumb, kid. This isn't recess for schoolchildren."

I save my clever rejoinder, knowing it will be wasted here. Instead, I hurl the blossom pod with all my might, straight for Talon Smithfield's ridiculously handsome face. At least, that is where I attempt to hurl it.

In actuality, it flies somewhere off to my left.

"HA!" Talon Smithfield laughs. "Nice try, kid!"

But the pod bounces off Peanut's box-shaped booty.

It sails through the air, rebounding off Sea-Monkey's roly-poly belly.

It soars to the right and ricochets off Tater Tot's head.

And creams Talon Smithfield right in the bean.

Talon stumbles backward in surprise. Tater Tot tilts her enormous nose-horn forward. She hooks the Taser and flings it skyward. Peanut deflects it with his agile posterior, sending it boomeranging straight into my hand.

"KAMIKAZE!!!"

Drumstick loops through Talon Smithfield's lanky legs. Talon sprawls backward and falls right into the waiting arms of Kou Kou. The panda bear-hugs him gently but firmly into submission.

I click the Taser. The air zaps with electrical sparks. I put my arm around Darvish. "Sorry to interrupt your conversation, Darvish, old boy, but I couldn't take any more talk. It was time for some action."

Darvish smiles and pulls his hand out of his pocket. "Oh, I think all that talk paid off pretty well," he says.

He's holding something in his hand. It is long. It is thin.

It is his spy pen. With built-in ultrasonic recording capability.

He's caught every word for digital posterity. I'm so proud. Hanging out with me has been good for him.

"You know what?" I say, realization dawning. "I'm starting to think that Haughtry Vain was never even involved in this at all."

Darvish slaps his palm to his forehead. Clearly, this revelation never even occurred to him.

Good old Darvish. Always two steps behind me.

Talon Smithfield struggles in Kou Kou's grasp, but it's obvious that he's going nowhere. "How did you do that?" he cries at me. "That was an impossible throw!"

I look around at my ghostly teammates and grin.

"I guess I'm just really good at dodgeball," I answer. "It's a curse."

36

When Darvish and I return to school the next day, we are met with far less pomp and circumstance than befits our courageous deeds of derring-do.

There is a deplorable lack of parades.

There is a disturbing absence of cheering.

There is a neglectful dearth of balloons.

Once again, my acts of responsibility, common sense, and valor will go unsung.

All that greets me is the sound of Sami Mulpepper reading her current event. And the internal pride of a job well done.

Sami reads, "'Middling Zoo Murders Solved under Strange Circumstances.

"'Zoo staff arrived early this morning to a surprising sight. They found a teenage male being firmly but gently hugged by Kou Kou the panda. At first, officials suspected the victim was a zoo visitor who had unknowingly fallen into the panda cage. However, further investigation revealed a set of missing zoo keys on his person, as well as a recording device containing his confession in the murders of four endangered animals at the Middling Zoo over the last month. The offender has been identified as one Talon Smithfield, former president of an organization known as PUPAE, People United to Protect Animals Everywhere.

"'The stolen keys belong to one Timothy Creskin, president of the zoo board.'"

"Oh my gosh!" cries Edwin Willoughby. "That's Holly's dad!"

I turn my gaze solemnly to Holly Creskin's empty chair. She has clearly stayed home today. She is a good egg, despite her overuse of perfume and dislike for dogs. I hope she does not suffer too much because of her father's scandalous predicament.

"Edwin, please don't interrupt Sami while she's reading her current event," says Ms. Yardley.

"Thank you, Ms. Yardley," coos Sami Mulpepper. She keeps reading.

"'Mr. Creskin is being questioned for possible connections to the case, but it does not seem that he was involved *in Mr. Smithfield's activities. Meanwhile, Mr. Smithfield faces criminal charges.'"*

Sami Mulpepper returns to her desk. "Hi, Rex," she whispers as she takes her seat.

"Um . . ." I say. Classic.

Ms. Yardley rises to her feet. "Great job, Sami. Does anyone else have a current event to share?"

If she only knew. If she only had the slightest inkling that heroism sits in her midst, fresh from the battlefield of bravery.

But, sadly, Ms. Yardley has no intuitive appreciation for the congratulatory brouhaha that is due. No sense of occasion. No realization that celebration is in order, with parades and cheering and balloons. No recognition that Darvish, even Darvish, deserves a few balloons of his own.

She only understands the rigors of her lesson plan. Which happens to contain a chilling fact that lets the air right out of my nonexistent balloons.

"Our final research report is due tomorrow," she says. "That's you, Rex. We look forward to hearing your oral report."

I'm unsure if a wicked grin flutters across her face or if it is a trick of the light. Either way, my stomach drops.

Because, in the hurly-burly of saving Middling Falls from the ravages of a deranged animal-murderer,

I have forgotten all about my report. And, to use the fraction vernacular of which Ms. Yardley is so fond, I have done zero-tenths of my research.

I haven't even picked a topic.

But, as has been my experience, flashes of inspiration often come unbidden. Research may be a necessary evil for the average Joe, but when you have *lived* the current events, research is just one more needless parlor trick.

I pull out my notebook and begin to write:

THE REAL STORY BEHIND THE
MIDDLING ZOO MURDERS
BY REX DEXTER

37

My oral report is a groundbreaking success.

Modesty prevents me from sharing the details. But I will tell you that my topic is inspired. My stage presence is the stuff of legends. My delivery makes one want to laugh and weep all in the same breath. My ending is innovative and avant-garde, with just a hint of folksy charm to satisfy the common man.

All in all, it is a triumph of unparalleled proportions.

But modesty prevents me from saying more on the subject, so quit asking.

Except that it is truly A+++ material.

Now, stop bringing it up. You're embarrassing me.

38

"**C**-plus?!" I exclaim.

It is an affront to nature and an indictment of the educational system in this country. Possibly several countries.

"I thought it was really good, Rex," says Darvish. He is sitting in my beanbag chair, munching on some type of seeds.

I stare at him. "Out of respect for my unfairly graded condition, can you at least snack on something normal? Cheetos, perhaps?"

The rhino, gorilla, shark, elephant, panda, and chicken are gathered around me like a Greek chorus. They alone seem to understand the injustice that has befallen me.

"She didn't like it?" asks Sea-Monkey.

I read Ms. Yardley's notes from my paper. "She says it was delivered with confidence and self-assurance, but the facts themselves seem unknowable by any public record. A for presentation, D minus for research."

I turn to them, agog. "She thinks I made this stuff up! She can't handle my insider information!"

Darvish shrugs. "Maybe that's best. Do you really want it to be widespread knowledge that you're talking to dead animals? It seems cuckoo to me, and I'm living it alongside you."

I made no mention of seeing or talking to dead animals in the report. Even so, Darvish speaks sense.

Still, the grade rankles my sense of fairness. It seems I am forever doomed to demonstrate untold responsibility, maturity, and common sense and receive no credit for it. Maybe I am expecting too much.

After all, there are those precious few that appreciate my efforts. I turn now to face them.

Peanut waddles his cube-shaped girth toward me. He caresses my cheek with his trunk. "Hey, now. Don't fret. Next time I see a trail of peanuts, I'll think before I follow them. You taught me that."

Mei Mei steps up to me, her Taser-fried hairdo going every which way. The panda no longer glows gold, but the look in her eyes sends tingles of warmth through my chest. "I am grateful to you, Rex Dexter," says Mei Mei, hugging me. "You saved Kou Kou. You made right a great wrong. You are my friend."

Sea-Monkey approaches me slowly, his deep brow raised high. "One time, I saw a tree frog fall seventeen stories from the forest canopy, colliding midair with a flying squirrel and hitting several sharp branches on the way down. I plucked it out of thin air at the last possible second, saving its miserable life."

He grins at me. "You did better than that."

"On my report?"

"On everything." He wraps his big, hairy gorilla arms around my neck.

The shark clears its throat pointedly. The gorilla nods, reaches around, and lifts the shark from his bottom.

"My dear boy," says the shark. "It has been a true delight knowing you. May I say, on behalf of my esteemed colleagues, how very grateful we are to you. You have done us all a tremendous service, and we are eternally thankful for the resolution you have brought to each of us."

My mouth hangs open.

Sea-Monkey puts the shark back on his butt where it belongs and it clamps on happily.

"Nobody else knows what you did," says the gorilla. "But we know."

The shark nibbles his rump with what I assume to be agreement.

Tater Tot nudges me softly with her crispy-fried nose-horn. "Wow. Just wow."

"What?" I ask.

She sniffles. "I'm really gonna miss you. That's what." She folds me warmly into her big rhino hug. "You did good," she whispers.

I choke back a sob. As I sink into the reassuring arms of a rhino, it hits me hard. I'm going to miss them, too.

"Do you have any soda?" squawks Darvish. "These chia seeds are making me constipated."

I glare in his direction. "Do you mind? I'm having a moment here."

"Well, how am I supposed to know? I can't see them!" He hangs his head and returns to his chia.

Yep, life is returning to normal.

But my dead pets are fading away. They slowly turn to mist before my eyes. I feel a lump rising in my throat. Somehow, I know I won't be seeing them again.

"Thank you, Rex," Tater Tot whispers.

And they are gone.

I sit down. I take a shaky breath and wipe my eyes. A bittersweet sadness washes over me. And with it, a sense of peace.

"Oh, are you done with your moment?" asks Darvish sarcastically. "Now can I have a soda?"

"Ooh! Soda!" says Drumstick. "Me too?"

Yep, he's still here. It seems the chicken has nowhere better to be.

I'm glad.

I shoot a grin at them. "Yes," I say. "You both definitely deserve a soda."

"Well, it's about time I get a little appreciation," says Darvish.

"Though let's be clear," I say. "A good sidekick

should avoid artificially sweetened drinks. Your blood sugar could drop right when I need you most."

"How many times do I have to tell you?" says Darvish. "I'm not your sidekick."

"I wasn't talking to you." I walk over to Drumstick, and we do a very complicated fourteen-step handshake.

I would teach it to you. But it's secret. Just for us second-best buddies.

39

I knew it would only be a matter of time before my mom and dad asked about my research report grade. And the day after my zoo pals have faded into oblivion, my fate has caught up with me.

I hold the paper out to them.

"C-plus?" says my mom. "Hmm."

"It's not great, Rex," says my dad. "But it's not terrible, either. Better than your last biology test."

"Ms. Yardley does say you demonstrated confidence and self-assurance," my mom concedes.

"That's really great," says my dad.

"The woman has it out for me," I explain. "It's not technically my—"

I stop myself. I look at the paper. Then back to them. "To be fair, I could have done more research."

They look at each other as if they are about to cry, which baffles me. I can't tell if they are happy or upset.

"That's a very mature way of looking at it," says my mom.

"I agree," says my dad. "Very responsible. You keep that up and maybe you'll be closer to getting that dog than you thought."

I get a C+ on my research report and they are ready to give me a dog.

Classic.

Enlightened or not, these people make no sense. But I have long since quit trying to unravel the mysteries of my parents.

"No hurry on the dog," I say. "Whenever you think the time is right."

Their mouths hang open in shock. I have rendered them speechless.

But the simple truth is, I'm no longer in a rush to get a chocolate Labrador.

I mean, I just spent the last couple weeks hanging out with a dead rhino and a dead elephant and a dead gorilla and a dead shark and a dead panda bear. After all that, a plain old dog seems kind of boring.

But my parents seem to attach bigger cosmic meaning to my statement. A meaning that appears to be making them weepy. Because Dad seems to have something in his eyes and Mom turns all misty and starts mumbling something about "growing up so fast!"

Grown-ups are so weird.

40

So that's it.

I told you that you probably wouldn't believe me. But it's all true.

Whether you believe this story or not, allow me to share a couple parting thoughts from my stockpile of worldly and otherworldly wisdom:

If you ever find yourself in Middling Falls, and you wander over to PetPlanet, you might come across an old, broken-down carnival game called *The Reaper's Curse*. It doesn't work anymore.

But if you can somehow miraculously get it going (they say peeing on the cord sometimes works), the bony dude inside is likely to challenge you to a bet. And if you lose, you're going to be cursed.

Two things worth noting:

1. Getting cursed by the Grim Reaper stinks big-time.
2. And then . . . somehow . . . it doesn't.

Oh, also . . . avoid Middling Falls altogether, if you can. It's really boring. Well, it used to be really boring. I confess, things have gotten more exciting lately.

Now, if you'll excuse me, my ride will be here soon. Sami Mulpepper and her mother are picking me up at any moment.

Oh, did I forget to mention? The Evening of Enchantment dance is tonight. My mom has acquired my turquoise corsage. Turns out, *corsage* is just a fancy word for *flower*. Who knew? Apparently, my mom. I suppose I could have looked it up. But my mind has been on other things.

The zoo is closed. Talon Smithfield is facing charges. The zoo board is under investigation. It seems almost frivolous to go to a dance when I am fresh from the trenches of righting so many wrongs. But I deserve an evening of enchantment. I have earned some rest and relaxation.

There is just one problem. I do not feel enchanted. I do not feel restful. I do not feel relaxed.

I feel like I might throw up.

Now that the moment is upon me, it occurs to me that there is one thing more nerve-racking than facing down six recently deceased ghost animals. And that thing is facing Sami Mulpepper in a blue-green ball gown. I do not know what was going through my mind when I agreed to undergo this ordeal.

Darvish is not going to the dance. That is because my best friend is a coward. Or a genius. I haven't decided which one.

But I have survived some truly alarming events in the last couple weeks. I will survive one evening of school-sanctioned merrymaking in a gymnasium.

And then I have stuff to do.

Serious stuff.

Significant stuff.

Stuff with real cosmic meaning.

Because, according to my dead chicken, there's a dead narwhal waiting in my beanbag chair.

And he probably needs my help.

ACKNOWLEDGMENTS

My name is on the front cover. But this is not just my book. There's a whole mess of people responsible for the story in your hands. Personally, I blame them.

I've listed some of the top culprits below. If there's anything you loved about this story, anything that made you laugh, anything that lifted you up from the humdrum day-to-day, now you know who to thank.

You're welcome.

But these guys really helped, too. A whole big bunch.

• Jodi Reamer, my agent, my friend, and my own personal Darvish. Or maybe I'm her Darvish. Or maybe one of us is the chicken. Regardless, I'm super thankful she's in my corner.

• Tracey Keevan, editor extraordinaire, who believed in this whackadoodle story, fought for it, breathed fresh life into it, and asked for two more just like it.

• Jamie Alloy, Melissa Lee, Esther Cajahuaringa, Christine Collins, and a whole squad of living, breathing, talented people at Disney Hyperion, who designed, marketed, and generally made this book so much cooler than I ever could.

• Hugo Cuellar, for his wonderfully weird illustrations.

• My dad, possibly my biggest fan, who is personally responsible for accosting far too many strangers on the streets to tell them about my books.

• Shelly, Reese, and Ethan. My crew. My team. My reason for writing. My inspiration for creating. If I was a dead gorilla with a dead shark attached to my heinie and I could pick anybody to haunt, it would totally be you three.

• And finally, the legions of incredibly kick-butt elementary school librarians I encounter on a regular basis. Thank you for putting my stories into kids' hands. It is a monumental pleasure to partner with you in our mission to create kids who love books.